MW00618167

ROYAL
COCKTAIL

Also by J. Kenner

The Fallen Saint Series

My Fallen Saint

My Beautiful Sin

My Cruel Salvation

Sinner's Game

The Stark Saga

Meet Damien Stark in the award-winning and internationally bestselling series that started it all...

He'd pay any price to have her...

release me

claim me

complete me

take me (novella)

have me (novella)

play my game (novella)

seduce me (novella)

unwrap me (novella)

deepest kiss (novella)

entice me (novella)

anchor me

hold me (novella)

please me (novella)

lost with me

damien

indulge me (novella)

delight me (novella & bonus content)

cherish me (novella)

embrace me (novella)

enchant me

Stark Security

Charismatic. Dangerous. Sexy as hell.

Shattered With You

Shadows Of You

(prequel to Broken With You)

Broken With You

Ruined With You

Wrecked With You

Destroyed With You

Memories of You (novella)

Ravaged With You

The Steele Books/Stark International:

He was the only man who made her feel alive.

Say My Name

On My Knees

Under My Skin

Stark International Novellas:

Meet Jamie & Ryan-so hot it sizzles.

Tame Me

Tempt Me

Tease Me

S.I.N. Trilogy:

It was wrong for them to be together…

…but harder to stay apart.

Dirtiest Secret

Hottest Mess

Sweetest Taboo

Most Wanted:

Powerful, dangerous, seductive

Wanted

Heated

Ignited

Stark World Stories:

Set in the Stark universe.

Wicked Grind

Wicked Dirty

Wicked Torture

Justify Me

The Fallen Saint Series

His touch is her sin. Her love is his salvation

My Fallen Saint

My Beautiful Sin

My Cruel Salvation

Man of the Month

Who's your man of the month …?

Down On Me

Hold On Tight

Need You Now

Start Me Up

Get It On

In Your Eyes

Turn Me On

Shake It Up

All Night Long

In Too Deep

Light My Fire

Walk The Line

Royal Cocktail (bonus book)

*Bar Bites: A Man of the Month Cookbook

Blackwell-Lyon:

Heat, humor & a hint of danger

Lovely Little Liar

Pretty Little Player

Sexy Little Sinner

Tempting Little Tease

Writing as Julie Kenner:

Rising Storm:

Small town drama

Rising Storm: Tempest Rising

Rising Storm: Quiet Storm

Demon Hunting Soccer Mom:

Paranormal women's fiction

Carpe Demon

California Demon

Demons Are Forever

Deja Demon

The Demon You Know (short story)

Demon Ex Machina

Pax Demonica

Day of the Demon

The Dark Pleasures Series:

Billionaire immortal romance

Caress of Darkness

Find Me In Darkness

Find Me In Pleasure

Find Me In Passion

Caress of Pleasure

For a complete booklist, visit www.jkenner.com

Praise for J. Kenner's Novels

"It is not often when a book is so amazingly well-written that I find it hard to even begin to accurately describe it . . . I recommend this book to everyone who is interested in a passionate love story." *Romancebookworm's Reviews (on Release Me)*

"A sizzling, intoxicating, sexy read!!!! J. Kenner had me devouring *Wicked Dirty* … With her sophisticated prose, Kenner created a love story that had the perfect blend of lust, passion, sexual tension, raw emotions and love." *Four Chicks Flipping Pages*

"I have read many J. Kenner's books, but this one has to be in my top 5. It was fast paced, suspenseful and HOT." *Read.Review.Repeat Blog (on Shattered With You)*

"With enough emotion to rip out your heart and the right amount of sexiness and intrigue to ramp up the excitement, *Broken With You* has to be one of my favorite J. Kenner novels to date." *Harlequin Junkie Blog*

J. KENNER

NEW YORK TIMES BESTSELLING AUTHOR

Cover design by Michele Catalano, Catalano Creative
Cover image from Deposit Photos by Tverdohlib.com

Published by Martini & Olive Books

V-2021-7-5D

ISBN:
Digital: 978-1-953572-21-9
Print: 978-1-953572-45-5

Chapter One

Two Years Ago

"OUT ALL NIGHT DRINKING? For pity's sake, Leopold, I thought you were there to study physics, not drink and screw around. And what happened to keeping a low profile?"

Prince Stephan Leopold of Avelle-am-see, Duke of Fluszbein, and heir to the throne, pressed his hands to his head as he sat up, groaning as the pounding headache rolled through him. He glanced at the clock and groaned again, regretting that he'd punched the speaker button and answered the phone. "Christ, Gisele, it's not even six here. And it was just a couple of drinks in a bar."

"Quatersh!" His sister spat out the word in their native Avellian tongue, a derivation of German and

Danish that was as old as their tiny European country.

"It's not nonsense," Leopold protested. "I went out to a local bar with a friend. We drank. We ate. We hung out. And it wasn't all night. Besides it's not like I'm prancing around Austin with a stein of beer in my hand."

"So the girl is no one special? Just another of your admirers ready to help you accelerate a few particles of your own?"

Leopold winced at the harsh tone and bad physics joke, though he should have expected them. He'd spent too many years partying with too many girls. But that was because he'd been trapped. Born into a role he didn't want, and he'd been acting out in the time-honored tradition of many a royal before him. With alcohol and sex.

Now was different. He'd begged his father to allow him to come to the States to study under Professor Malkin. And now that he was here, he not only wanted to keep a low profile so that his father didn't decide to call him home, but he had no interest in meaningless flings to dull the pain of his future. Not when he was so deeply invested in his present.

So far, it seemed to have worked. He was incognito in the States, going by Leo instead of his given name, and adding a surname though he didn't formally have one at home. He was using Stahl, the name of one branch of his mother's family.

His goal had been to avoid the public eye that so enjoyed focusing on the supposed glamour of royal life. And since his country was small, Leopold had actually managed to stay off the radar these last few months, something his British cousins never seemed to manage.

"Sire?"

He grimaced. "Do not call me that. I do not sit on the throne." *Yet.*

"I was asking about the girl. Who is she?"

A vision of her quick smile and thoughtful brown eyes came into his head. Her chin-length honey-brown hair tucked behind one ear. Her soft skin. And the way her lips had tasted when he'd so gently kissed her.

"*Leopold.* Who is she?"

He jumped. "Just a girl." *Lie.* "A law student." *Truth.*

Gisele stayed silent.

Leopold cleared his throat and continued. "We were hanging with a group of friends." *Also truth.* "And how did you know, anyway? I—"

He cut himself off. "*Jürgen.*" Leopold snapped out the name of his personal bodyguard, the man who headed the small security detail that had come with him from Avelle-am-see to the University of

Texas and who was expected to serve and protect the heir. "I swear, I'm docking that man's pay."

"Then it's fortunate for Jürgen that you're not the Chancellor of the Exchequer. And this isn't the point. Do you really think that Father will let you stay in Texas if he learns of this behavior?"

"There was no *behavior*. As I said, she is only a friend."

The first statement was sadly true. Despite the intense and surprising connection he'd felt to the woman he'd first caught sight of in the local bar, theirs wasn't a relationship that could go anywhere. He was the heir to the throne. Destined to marry a citizen of his country or another royal. A wife he didn't want, to go with the job he didn't want.

Was it any wonder he sometimes escaped to find solace in a round of drinks and a bevy of gorgeous women?

But that wasn't Skye. She could never be his, and yet he craved and respected her in a way he'd never felt before. And, he feared, would never feel again.

"Just be careful, little brother. Father only agreed to let you go in the first place because of the opportunity to do some graduate work under Professor Malkin. Father knows how much it means to you."

Leopold snorted.

"Don't be like that. He conceded a lot. He

recognizes that the sciences are important to the realm, and that your reign will impact the direction our country goes."

She was right, of course. Increasing the scientific relevancy of their country had been one of Leopold's pet projects since he was twelve and had accompanied his father on a diplomatic trip to the CERN Large Hadron Collider in neighboring Switzerland. The world was changing so fast, and he wanted his country to move purposefully into the future while maintaining the traditions of the past that kept their homeland so beautiful and charming.

What he didn't want was the throne.

Leopold knew he could rule. His entire childhood had been a virtual schoolroom on diplomacy and how to lead a country. But it didn't come naturally. Not the way physics and chemistry did. Not the way leadership came to Gisele, who would be a brilliant and beloved queen. She might be a pain in his ass, but his sister was truly remarkable.

But she was born a woman, and though she was the firstborn and three years his senior, the country's ancient rule of agnatic primogeniture had been included in their constitution when it was adopted over a century ago.

It wasn't fair, but very little about the life of a royal was. The world saw fame and privilege and servants and castles. All that was true, of course, but what most of the world didn't see was the path. A golden road illuminated by intrusive spotlights and lined with chains, from which he was not allowed to stray. Maybe that was starting to change, but not fast enough to suit Leopold. And not fast at all in his small country.

And yet King Wilhelm had allowed him this small bit of freedom.

He sighed, feeling like a dick. Gisele was right. Their father understood the pressures and sacrifices of being a royal. And while Father fully intended to prepare the prince to rule the country one day, he also saw Leopold as a man, not just a royal. And because of that, he'd not only forgiven Leopold's rebellious teenage years, he'd consented to letting Leopold study in Texas under the renowned quantum physicist, Jeffrey Malkin.

Leopold had assured his father he would behave, and yet last night he'd slipped away from Jürgen to go meet Skye. Or, at least, he'd thought he'd given his bodyguard the slip.

"We were just having a drink," he told his sister. "Truly. It wasn't a social media event. No one here even knows who I am."

"My point is that it needs to stay that way. You start prancing around with this girl, and suddenly—"

"I told you. She's just a friend." He fought back a wince as he spoke the lie, his chest tightening with the memory of the brush of her lips over his skin. His pulse raced every time he touched her. Hell, every time he looked at her. She was a friend, sure. But even though they'd only met one short week ago, she'd already become so much more than that.

But no way was he sharing that fact with his sister.

Secrets.

He swallowed, feeling their weight.

The secret he kept from his sister about the woman he craved.

The secret he kept from Skye about who he really was.

He was navigating rocky terrain, and all he could do was hope that he didn't lose his footing.

Chapter Two

Present Day

"I … can't believe he's … doing … this to me." Skye Porter concentrated on speaking slowly, tears close to the surface. She took the last swallow of her whiskey sour—because today called for something stronger than her usual wine—then met Hannah's eyes. "Doesn't he get it?"

"He loves you, Skye. You know that."

Skye shook her head, emotion pooling in her gut. Disagreement. Displeasure. Something like that, anyway. She turned in her seat, glancing around the friendly, cozy bar where they often met after work. It was warm and inviting. A welcoming place. The perfect place to come on a day like today when her work had gone completely off the rails.

All her life, Skye had wanted to be a particular

kind of appellate lawyer. The kind who dug deep into theory and precedent. Who wrote briefs that swayed judges and changed history. Important work where she could live in a library with her books and thoughts, letting another lawyer actually stand up and make the oral argument, because no way did Skye want to be in that spotlight.

It was her ideal job, a dream she'd worked toward since childhood. And for the last two years she'd been walking on a cloud because she'd been living that dream.

Today, with a single announcement, her father had twisted that dream into a nightmare.

Hannah leaned forward, then reached across the small two-top to put a consoling hand over Skye's. She gave a little squeeze. "You know I'm right."

Skye exhaled, reconciling herself to the truth. "About loving me? I guess." Words never came easy, but they were downright stubborn when she was agitated. *Breathe.* She took a breath, then another before continuing. "But he should have asked." More than that, he shouldn't have needed to ask. He should have known that her answer would be no.

"It's not about … love," Skye continued. She concentrated on speaking slowly, using all the techniques she'd been taught over the years, but hating the inevitable stops and starts between her words. "It's—it's about … fixing me."

"You're not broken." Hannah's words lashed out at Skye, and she immediately wanted to hug her friend for being so damn loyal even as she wanted to chastise her for being a naive idiot.

Because no matter what her friends or therapists said, Skye *was* broken. She'd been broken since she was five. Her brain banged and bruised in the same accident that had killed her mother.

"He thinks…" She trailed off, waiting for Hannah to lift her head and look at Skye's face. It was always easier for people to understand her gravel-laden voice and slow, muddy words if they were both watching and listening. "He thinks that if this group understands me, then everything is just fine. And that … will ease his guilt."

A presentation to a conference room full of international big wigs. General counsel for major corporations. Government leaders. Entrepreneurs and philanthropists. All potential clients of the firm coming to a day-long symposium, and Tarlton Anderson Porter had signed her up to speak to the group.

Had her father lost his freaking mind?

"He'll always feel guilty," Hannah said gently. "It doesn't matter that the truck blew through a red light. He was the one driving the car."

Hannah was right, of course. Skye's mother had

died in that accident, and Skye had come close. She'd spent almost two months in the hospital. And despite her father's fortune, no doctor could fix her.

And though her father had walked away from the accident with nothing more serious than a broken arm, Skye knew that he was as damaged as she was.

Before the accident, she'd been a chatterbox. Everyone said so. After—well, after, she hated the way she sounded. The way she couldn't control how her mouth moved and couldn't predict how the words would come out.

Traumatic brain injury. And it wasn't the kind of thing that would ever completely heal.

Those sluggish and muddled words had become a part of her, and not a part she liked. She tried to breathe properly. To force the words to come slowly. But even with years of practice, it was hard. Most of the time, she sounded drunk, her speech slurred and her cadence off. And repeating things because people didn't understand was her personal nightmare.

She knew she should be grateful that only her speech was impacted. But getting good grades was cold comfort, especially when both kids and adults would hear her speak and just assume she was below the line academically. Standing to present in front of the class had brought on sweats and shakes and only made her already thick speech that much worse. She'd had to prove herself over and over so many times that she'd been utterly exhausted—not to mention relieved—when she graduated.

She might be out of school now, but she was still self-conscious around everyone except her family and the co-workers she knew best.

Her father understood all that. He'd lived the daily drama with her. And yet here he was, throwing her out into the world. A world where people weren't used to deciphering the cadence and slur of her speech.

"Just tell him no," Hannah said gently.

Skye shook her head. The advice was great in theory, but total crap in practice. Tarlton Porter was one of the firm's senior partners, the grandson of one of the founders, and the head of the Austin office of Porter, Jenson & Kaye. He was a man whose praise of a new attorney could push their career up a notch, and whose sidelong glance of displeasure had sent more than one young associate racing toward the restroom with a sour stomach churning with nerves. Such a common reaction, in fact, that all the restrooms were stocked with a mouthwash dispenser.

Just because he was her father didn't make Skye immune to the Tarlton Effect. So there was no way she was walking into his office and telling her dad that she wanted him to assign someone else to present her paper at the symposium.

Even if she could ask him without nausea and weak knees, it would be career suicide. More than that, it would make for a very un-merry Christmas. Never mind that it was still summer. Tarlton Porter, Esq. knew how to hold a grudge.

She shook her head, wanting to cry. Like seriously, truly, honestly wanting to just break down in tears. A presentation to over a hundred big wigs from all over the globe. People with massive influence, who expected presentations to be both polished and understandable.

Well, they were in for a shock when *she* slid behind that microphone. She drew in a shaky breath. "I need a way out of this. But short of emergency … surgery or running away to Australia, there is no way." She blinked back tears. "You know he won't let me back out and … and I don't want to disappoint him." The tears flowed freely now. "But I will. You know … I will."

She shuddered, and Hannah reached over and squeezed her hand again. "I really am sorry. But maybe it won't be as bad as you think."

"It will." Skye was certain of that. "And don't tell me … you can understand me. That's not the point." She was suddenly aware of the way she was concentrating on her breathing. The effort required simply to try, often futilely, to keep her speech understandable. It was exhausting. And her dad thought she could present an entire paper?

"He thinks that if he just pushes the right buttons … then everything will be better. But this is me."

"I think that's the point, Skye. All your dad wants is for you to be you."

Skye waved the words away. "Wasn't traffic a bitch today?"

Hannah stared at her for a moment, then burst out laughing. "Is that your subtle cue that it's time to change the subject?"

"It wasn't meant … to be subtle at all."

"Fine." Hannah finished off her drink, then signaled to Tyree, the bar's owner and a friend, for the check. "We'll change the subject to Bart."

Skye frowned. "What about him?"
Bartholomew Greene was a friend from law school who was currently crashing at her place while his house was being remodeled.

"That's my question," Hannah said, a lascivious edge to her voice.

"We're … just friends." He was one of her best friends, actually. Someone who knew her secrets and had her back. But their connection had never been sexual or romantic. Which made him the perfect roommate.

"Uh-huh…"

"I'm serious," Skye said, wishing she could make her voice sound more emphatic. "He'd tell you the same."

"Fine."

A waitress Skye had never seen before dropped the bill off at their table, and Hannah immediately reached for it.

Skye shook her head. "You listened to my pity party. I'll pay."

"Fair enough," Hannah said, then pushed the bill toward Skye. "As for Bart, all I'm saying is that you haven't dated since *him*." She shot a quick glance toward the bulletin board that boasted dozens of candid shots of male customers alongside the twelve winners of the bar's original Man of the Month contest. Once upon a time, *his* picture had been among the candid photos. At least until Skye had ripped it off in fury when she'd learned the truth.

"Two years and no sex," Hannah chirped. "I'm just pointing that out."

"Hannah, don't." Not a day went by that Skye didn't think about Leo, the first man she'd loved. The *only* man she'd loved. "Please … don't." Her voice sounded even more slurred than usual, because her throat was thick with tears.

Across the table, Hannah's shoulders fell. "I'm sorry. I wasn't thinking. I was—"

"It's fine." She concentrated on pulling out enough cash to leave on the table so that she had an excuse not to meet Hannah's eyes. Then she pushed her chair back. "Ready?"

"You go on," Hannah said. "I'm meeting Matthew here as soon as he finishes his last training session for the day."

Skye nodded, pushing down the rising jealousy. The owner of an Austin-based chain of gyms, Matthew Herrington was Hannah's husband, and after a crazy start with a fake engagement, now they were about as happy as a couple could be. Skye adored them both, but some days it was just plain hard being around them. Because more and more she feared that she'd never find that kind of love.

Not the kind that lasted, anyway.

She reached for her purse, slung it over her shoulder, and told Hannah she'd check in tomorrow. Then she gave Tyree a quick wave followed by a nod to Jenna, one of the owners who was hurrying toward the back office with a baby on her hip.

Other than her office, The Fix on Sixth was one of the few places where Skye didn't feel awkward speaking because both the staff and the regulars had come to know her over the years. She smiled to herself as she walked toward the entrance, remembering *Cheers,* the classic TV show that she used to watch with her dad. The Fix on Sixth was definitely a place where everyone knew her name.

She was glancing around as she walked, waving at a few familiar faces, and not paying enough attention to where she was going. Which was why she almost barreled straight into the tall, dark-haired man with broad shoulders, the delicious scent of sandalwood soap, and the familiar, kissable mouth with parted lips now forming a startled *oh.*

"Skye?"

She froze. And for one glorious moment, joy spiraled through her.

Then reality came crashing back, and without even thinking, she lashed out and slapped Prince Stephan Leopold, heir to the crown of Avelle-am-see, hard across the face.

Chapter Three

Two Years Ago

ANTITRUST LAW WAS THE WORST. Or maybe it was just her professor who was the worst.

Either way, it didn't matter. Because unless Skye Porter managed to wrap her head around his nonsensically meandering lectures, she was going to fail and ruin her straight-A average right as she was heading into her last year of law school. Which would be fine if she wanted to go straight into practicing. Her GPA would still be plenty high. But she wanted to clerk for a year on an appellate court, then return to work at Porter, Jenson & Kaye, the firm her great-grandfather had co-founded in New York over a century before. And appellate clerkships were incredibly competitive.

She sighed, the thick, blue-bound antitrust

treatise sitting open in front of her on the Tarlton Law Library table. She scowled at it, then went back to taking notes. If the adjunct professor teaching the class couldn't bother to organize his thoughts and actually teach, then she'd just have to huddle down with her casebook and a treatise and teach herself.

No matter what, she intended to ace this final. She drew a breath, flipped the page, and started taking more notes.

"Hey!"

Skye jumped a mile, then collapsed with a groan. "Hannah! You scared … me to death."

"Sorry about that." Her friend pulled out a chair and sat opposite Skye. She was older than Skye's twenty-four years, with an athletic build and blond hair that framed her face and brushed her shoulders. They'd met when Hannah did a summer clerkship at Porter, Jenson & Kaye while Skye was working as a lowly file clerk. Despite the fact that Skye had barely been out of high school, they'd had lunch a few times and stayed in touch. Now Hannah had her own firm, and Skye could think of only one reason why she'd be back in these hallowed halls.

"What are you researching?" Most law firms had their own basic libraries and online database access, but for obscure case law or scholarly articles that weren't easily found online, local attorneys often braved the parking situation and came to the University of Texas campus.

"No research," Hannah said. "I've been mentoring some 2Ls in the mock trial program. I saw you, and figured it was fate."

"Fate?"

"Absolutely. It's Friday. We should go get a drink at The Fix."

Skye cocked her head and stared down her friend. "We did that last night." She tried not to sigh with the memory. Because last night, *he* had been there.

He was the cute guy that Skye had caught looking at her for most of last night. Except *cute* wasn't the right word at all. For that matter, cute was an insult for this guy. He was magazine cover spectacular. Broad shoulders, a tight ass. Dark, thick hair with just a hint of wave to it. And his eyes...

Eyes so blue that she could see their color from all the way across the room. They were deep set and sexy, and every time his eyes caught hers, she felt hypnotized, and not in a bad way.

He had the face of a god, too, which made her want to keep looking. High cheekbones and an angular jaw line that inspired her to sketch him, and she didn't even know how to draw. As for his lips, well, they looked positively kissable.

All in all, looking at him had been like eating a sumptuous meal. And every time she'd taken a bite, he was looking right back at her, devouring her with his eyes.

The whole night had been weirdly sensual, and she wasn't sure if she was the only one who felt it, or if he did too. Either way, it was one of the sexier experiences in her life. And she couldn't deny that the possibility of seeing him again intrigued her more than it should.

"Come on, Skye. Why not? Are you saying we can't go two nights in a row?"

Skye shook off the memory. "I'm saying that Matthew must be out of town if you're looking to hang with me on a Friday night." Matthew and Hannah hadn't been together that long, but Skye had a feeling they'd be married soon. They fit together perfectly. She sighed, wondering if she'd ever find a guy she connected to like that.

His image popped into her mind, and she chastised herself. The guy was cute, and she'd felt a tug, but the odds of her ever seeing him again were slim, so…

"— in Dallas. He'll be back tomorrow afternoon."

Skye straightened, realizing she'd lost the thread of the conversation. "I'm sorry. What? Matthew's in Dallas?"

Hannah nodded. "I could have gone with him, but I had a hearing this morning and the mock trial thing just now." She sighed dramatically. "I'm so damn proud of how fast his business is expanding, but he's gone and now you're making me spend the evening alone, wallowing with Oreos and bad television."

"Can't have that. I guess we can … go to The Fix, and you can wallow … with fried food and tempting libations." And, bonus, maybe she really would see *him* again. A girl could hope.

She sighed as her mind conjured him … then caught the way Hannah was studying her. "What?"

"Nothing," Hannah said, her voice rising with mock innocence. "Just thinking what you're thinking."

Skye shook her head. "You are *so* not reading my mind."

"You mean you're not thinking that he might be there again, and that he's ridiculously cute, and this time, maybe you'll work up the nerve to talk to him?"

Skye shook her head, her heart pounding so hard she knew better than to even try talking.

"Careful," Hannah said. "You wouldn't want to ruin your profile."

Skye cocked her head, confused.

"Your nose is growing," Hannah said, then pushed back from the table. "I'll see you there at eight." Then she wiggled her fingers, turned, and walked away without waiting for Skye to answer.

Chapter Four

THE UBER DROPPED her off at the corner of Sixth and Congress, and Skye glanced around downtown Austin as she waited for the light to change. Her condo was only a few blocks away, and for a moment, she considered going straight home. She enjoyed The Fix—it was one of the few places in town where she didn't feel completely self-conscious—but she really did need to study. She ought to text an apology to Hannah, tell her she'd stayed at school too late, and just go home.

But she didn't.

She loved her condo, although technically it was her dad's. An investment property he'd bought over a decade ago. Originally, she'd worked up the courage to share a house with some other students who'd been matched during first year orientation. But when her dad offered to let her have the condo rent-free, she'd jumped at the chance. Not only did her place have a gorgeous view of the river, but she was living alone, which meant she didn't have to speak in front of strangers.

At the time, relief had flooded through her. Now, she regretted the decision. With her hesitancy to speak much and the long hours of studying, plus the travel back and forth from campus to downtown, she hadn't made many friends in law school.

If she'd agreed to share the house, maybe by now she'd have a group of friends to study with. Or at least to share a late-night movie marathon. But she'd chickened out, and for the most part, law school was a solo journey for her.

Still, she *did* have some friends, and one of them was waiting for her at The Fix on Sixth.

The light changed, and she crossed Congress Avenue, heading east toward the bar and away from her condo. She'd just crossed Brazos when her phone pinged. She glanced down and saw that the text was from Hannah.

Matthew surprised me by coming home early. Getting naked and blowing you off. XXOO

Skye shook her head at the irony, then frowned, pausing outside the wooden doors that led into The Fix. She was happy for Hannah, but the idea of going to a bar alone didn't appeal to her. Sure, she liked the staff, and after coming to The Fix regularly for more than two years, she felt mostly comfortable talking to them. But they'd be working. And Skye was the last person in the world who wanted to strike up a conversation with a stranger.

Still, she'd come all this way…

She reached for the door, hesitated, and changed her mind. A crowded bar on a Friday night where strangers would be mingling and talking? Definitely *not* the kind of stress she needed going into the weekend. Besides, she really should be thinking about antitrust law.

As she took a step backward, the door opened outward and she stumbled. She registered a blur of motion, then a firm, strong hand closing around hers, pulling her upright and steadying her.

"I am so sorry." The voice was deep and male, with an accent she couldn't place. "I wasn't looking where I—"

He lifted his head, met her eyes, and stopped speaking. *The guy from last night.*

"You." Her heart pounded against her ribs, and once again she felt as if she might topple over.

"Funny," he said in that adorable accent. "I was just going to say that." He stepped all the way out, the doors closing behind him as they lingered on the sidewalk.

"You were … looking at me." The words came out slow and thick, her speech more distorted than usual. Which, of course, made her want to go hide under the nearest rock. "Last … night," she added, feeling like an idiot, and wishing she'd just kept her mouth shut.

"I was looking at you?" The corner of his mouth twitched, and those blue eyes lit with humor. "I believe it was you doing the looking."

Clearly he'd had no trouble understanding her, and if he found her speech impediment annoying, he hid it well. Skye had to fight a ridiculously stupid grin as she said, "Oh … no. You were the one looking. For sure."

"Do I seem like the kind of man who would be so impolite as to ogle a beautiful woman?"

"Um, yeah." She grinned. He matched her smile, and it made him so handsome, her knees went a little weak.

"It's like you already know me," he said, and this time she couldn't stop the laughter.

Banter. She was actually bantering with this guy. How had that happened?

"Why don't we split the difference and say that we were looking at each other?"

"Yes," she said, managing to control her giggles. "I can … live with … that."

He turned toward the door, and she wanted the ground to swallow her up, since he was obviously now making a quick getaway. But then he flashed that smile again. "You were on your way in, weren't you?"

"I—yes. I mean, no."

"Well, that's rather confusing, isn't it?"

She cleared her throat and concentrated on speaking slowly and breathing properly. Usually she didn't have to focus so much, but he made her unreasonably nervous. "I was going to meet a friend. But she cancelled on me."

"So you were going to leave and deny those of us in the bar the pleasure of seeing you?"

"You were leaving, too."

"Something I never would have contemplated had I known you were about to enter."

"You're sweet." She looked down to hide both her blush and her nerves. "But … I should go. I have … finals coming up, and—"

"What are you studying?"

It was a common enough question, almost the equivalent of "How's it going." But he seemed genuinely interested.

"Law."

"Really? I wouldn't have taken you for a lawyer last night." His head tilted slightly as he looked at her, a frown tugging at the corners of his mouth. "Actually, maybe I would have."

"Why?"

"You looked like you were debating. That was one of the things that kept drawing my eyes back to you."

She'd been with Hannah and her law partner, Easton, both of whom Skye was comfortable speaking around. That, however, did not make for an accurate first impression. "I … don't usually talk that … much."

"Really? I'm surprised."

He spoke with no irony at all, but the words were just too much. The man wasn't deaf, which meant he had to be pulling her chain, and that pissed her off.

"Surprised? Then … you … are an … idiot." She turned away and started down the sidewalk. *What the hell?* It was one thing to ignore her speech. Another altogether to mock it.

She'd only gone five steps when he moved in front of her, blocking her path. "Please forgive me. That came out terribly wrong."

She considered pushing him aside—after all, she didn't know this guy and owed him nothing—but she heard real mortification in that polished voice.

She nodded, quick and sharp. "Apology accepted. Please … move."

"I only meant that you looked as if you were having a real conversation, not just random bar talk. I took you as a woman who goes deeper than small talk. I didn't mean to mock your speech. Is it dysarthria?"

Her spine went straight. "You know that?"

"My uncle was thrown from a horse when he was fifteen. He was treated, of course, and had regular therapy. And though there was some improvement in the early years, he never regained what most people would call normal speech." He smiled warmly at her. "He had his own normal, and though we could hear the difference, it bothered no one. The family was very matter-of-fact about his speech, and to be honest no one outside the family would have thought of teasing him or looking down on him because of it."

"Oh." Outside group therapy as a child and some volunteer work she did in a nursing home with stroke survivors, she'd never met anyone else with the condition. "What did he do for a living?"

"He was an advisor in, ah, the family business. He spoke quite a bit. Made presentations. That kind of thing. It was both a public and important job."

"I was five," she said, the words surprising her. "A car wreck. It … killed my mother."

"I'm so sorry."

"Thank you. And—well, I'm sorry I … snapped."

"No, I was insensitive." He tilted his head in a small nod, the gesture seeming both charming and old-fashioned. "So the man at your table yesterday…."

"Yes?"

"When the woman with you left, you and he seemed more … engaged."

"Oh, no. I'm not getting … married."

He chuckled, and her face burned as she realized he didn't mean *that* kind of engaged.

Thankfully it was too dark for him to see her cheeks, and she started walking again. Fast.

"No, no," he said, hurrying to catch up "I meant that the conversation seemed intense." He paused. "You're really not seeing him? Or anyone?"

She slowed her pace, shaking her head as she looked sideways at him. "We were making plans. For Hannah's birthday. Nothing more."

The corner of his mouth curved up in the most adorable grin. "Well, that's good information to have, isn't it?"

"Is it?" Her voice sounded breathy.

"Have you ever heard of quantum entanglement?"

She made a whooshing motion over her head.

He waved the words away. "Sorry. Not important. Let's just say you caught my eye."

She wanted to press him to tell her more, but she knew enough to know that he was talking physics. And frankly, a science lecture wasn't the direction she wanted this conversation to go. Not law, either, for that matter.

Rational thought warred with desire, and she hugged herself, wanting to join him for a drink, but also terrified by the idea. She didn't date much—

hell, she didn't date at all—and right before finals hardly seemed like the time to start.

She cleared her throat, determined to stay focused. "I should get home." A group of three drunk guys stumbled by, all ogling her and whistling. Harmless, but annoying. She ignored them, her attention still on her companion. "I've got finals soon."

Disappointment registered on his face, but he only nodded, then extended his hand. "I'll walk you to your car."

"My condo's close. I'm fine."

His attention cut back toward the three drunken guys, then returned to her. "Then I'll walk you to your door."

"You don't have to do that."

"No, but I know how daunting it can be to feel like you're being watched. Like you can't go from one place to another safely. Please, let me escort you."

She realized he spoke with an exactness to his words. His voice polished and careful. "Why do you know that?" she asked as they walked slowly down the street.

"Let's just say I've had an interesting life."

"You're too young to have completely had a life yet."

"I'm twenty-six. So let's say that I've had an interesting life so far."

She nodded slowly. "Are your parents celebrities?"

"Something like that."

"That must be hard," she said. "Being in the spotlight. They chose it, but you didn't. But ultimately, you'll … have your own life."

"Perhaps. Perhaps not. I come from a very traditional family," he said, "but I also know that we're very old school. And definitely an anomaly compared to most of the population."

She was about to ask what he meant when he continued.

"And you? Were you born into a family of lawyers? Or have you chosen this path?"

"Both. My great-grandfather founded a firm. I'll join, but only if my grades … are up to the firm's standards. And only … after I clerk for a judge."

"You're not willing to just skate because you're family."

He said it with approval, and she stood a little taller, amazed that he recognized that in her. And liked it.

"What if you didn't want to be a lawyer?" he asked as they approached the cross street. "What if you truly didn't want to, but you absolutely had to?"

The question was so surprising that she actually stumbled to a stop, then looked him up and down. She had no idea why he was asking it. He might simply be making conversation, but somehow she doubted it.

She licked her lips, not sure what the best answer would be, so she said the only true thing that came to mind. "My family wouldn't do that to me." But even as she said the words, she wondered if they were true. Her father had aspirations for her, after all.

"Pretend."

She frowned but tried to really think about the question. "I … I don't know. I wouldn't want to let them down, but…"

She trailed off with a shrug, and he nodded.

"Exactly," he said. "But."

For a moment, they stood in silence, then his lips curved in a slow smile. "Will you do me a favor?"

She swallowed, feeling a little excited, a little nervous. She had the strange realization that she'd been flirting, something that had never come naturally to her, but it felt good with this guy. Easy. "I don't know. What's the favor?"

"Will you turn around and let me buy you a drink?"

She thought of finals coming up. About how she'd been almost relieved that Hannah had bailed on her, because she needed to go lock herself in her apartment, curl up in bed with a mug of coffee and her antitrust book and learn everything she could.

She had things to do, law to learn, concepts to evaluate and turn over in her head until they made sense and felt like a part of her. It was important stuff. Important to her grade and the career she so desperately craved.

But she knew other things were important too, and for some inexplicable reason, she thought that this guy might be one of those things. "I'm Skye," she said.

"Leo. And is that a yes?"

She nodded, and when he took her hand, it felt like the start of something wonderful.

Chapter Five

"I GUESS THIS IS OUR PLACE," Skye said, after he'd urged her to blow off studying and head back to the bar.

They were standing just inside The Fix on Sixth, looking in at the large room filled with talking, laughing people gathered near the Austin, Texas, mural or sitting at the long, oak bar that ran along the west wall.

"I guess it is," he said, surprised by the butterflies in his stomach that had flapped into motion at the thought of him and Skye having their own place. "And it looks like we have a welcoming committee."

She turned her head to look at him quizzically, and he nodded across the room to the broad-shouldered man in a hoodie. The man's shadowed eyes narrowed as his head cocked to the side as if in question.

"Oh, that's Griffin," Skye told him. "He's a writer. He … camps out here a lot when he's not traveling."

"And he's staring me down because…?" Leopold hoped she had an answer. That this man had an unrequited, but completely understandable crush on Skye, for example. What he didn't want to learn was that Griffin had recognized him and was about to post a royal sighting on Twitter.

"He might be … worried about me."

Leopold frowned. "Because I look like a dangerous psycho?"

Her laugh delighted him. "No. Because he … might have noticed me looking at you last night." Her cheeks bloomed a delightful shade of pink. "He's probably checking up on me."

"Oh." Leopold nodded. "Well, I can't fault a friend for that."

"Do you mind?" She took a single step away from him, and he felt her absence immediately. The reaction was surprising—and entirely pleasant. "He knows … I should be studying. He probably … thinks you're a bad influence."

"That's what my family is always saying," he admitted. "I'm the original bad boy."

She bit her lip as she studied him, and it took all

his effort not to take a nip himself. "I'm not sure I believe that," she finally said. "But if you are … that could be fun, too."

Her blush deepened, and he grinned. Somehow he had a feeling that this girl was not the kind to fall for bad boys, and he had a sudden quick stab of regret for all the times that he'd gone a little wild back home.

"I'll be right back," she promised, then squeezed his fingers before crossing the bar, the warmth of her touch lingering with her lavender scent.

He watched her go, surprisingly relieved to have a moment to gather himself. He was undeniably nervous. Him.

It was ridiculous. He met regularly with heads of state and never had butterflies. He was raised to not be nervous. Other people were supposed to be nervous around him. He wasn't meant to feel this way. And yet there it was, impossible to miss. Sweaty palms. And those butterflies in his stomach that suggested that whatever he was doing with her was the most important thing in the world.

Leopold settled himself at a table and ordered them both Loaded Coronas. Then he leaned back and searched the bar. She was still there, talking with the writer who kept sneaking glances at Leopold from under that hoodie.

He sipped his drink, enjoying the taste of the beer mixed with rum. As he swallowed, he watched Skye, fascinated by her.

He'd never been attracted to a woman at first sight. He could appreciate a woman, of course, but there'd never been this kind of attraction. He tried to tell himself that it wasn't real. That this was simply a product of him not having dated in a while.

Somehow, he didn't believe that.

From across the room, Skye caught his eye and waved, then held up two fingers, presumably meaning she'd be back in two minutes. Not a problem. He was content to sip his beer and watch her.

He frowned, feeling eyes on him. Then he turned and saw Jürgen.

The man did his job well, Leopold had to give him that. He'd known the bodyguard had been shadowing them as they walked, and it was to Jürgen's credit that Leopold was able to completely erase the man from his mind.

He lifted his drink in a subtle toast, and grinned when Jürgen toasted him right back, then tilted his head toward Skye and gave him a small thumbs up.

Leopold rolled his eyes and turned back to the table, but he was more pleased by the approval than he should be.

He glanced at the menu, wondering what kind

of appetizers she'd like. When he looked up again, he didn't see her. A chill shot through his entire body, the fear that she had decided to leave. That her friend had told her that it was a bad idea to go out for drinks with a guy she barely knew, or that she'd found another guy she wanted to be with more.

He felt panic rise, and the Crown Prince of Avelle-am-see did not panic. Except, apparently, he did.

Then he saw her, and the world leveled again. He took a long sip of his drink, finishing off the bottle, and leaned back before signaling for another. This was not good. He barely knew this woman. So why was he letting her get under his skin this way?

The answer became clear when she came back to the table, smiling and laughing.

He was letting her in because he wanted to. Wanted *her*. Not forever—he knew well enough that couldn't happen. But for right now, he wanted to be with her. Not sex—at least not necessarily. But her. He didn't understand why, but she brought a wild joy into his life. The kind that he felt when he was working an equation and making progress, only more intense. And that kind of feeling was to be cherished.

"I love these," she said as she picked up the Loaded Corona and slid into the seat across from him. From what he could tell, she wasn't the least bit self-conscious about her speech around him anymore. "Thank you."

"You're welcome." He lifted his empty bottle. "I love them too."

"I'm sorry I disappeared. Griffin's overly … protective of me."

"He's a good friend."

"It's more than that. He was in … a fire, and his face is pretty scarred. So he—"

"I understand," he said gently. "He knows what it's like to be self-conscious."

She nodded. "And to be looked at like there's … something wrong with … you. Like you're less."

"Anyone who thinks that about you is an idiot."

She met his eyes. Held them. "That's what he says."

"Then I'll like your friend just fine."

She took a long sip of her drink then put it on the table. Then she reached over and took his hand, and it was as if the heavens opened.

He drew in a shaky breath, and met her eyes again, then felt as if he was drowning in those deep, brown pools. And, oh God, that shock of electricity that had cut through him with more intensity than anything he'd ever felt in his life.

She gasped, and he knew she felt it, too, as she held his gaze and said, very simply, "Hey."

"Hey, yourself."

For a moment, they just stared. Then, as if on cue, they grinned at each other.

Their stupid lack of words didn't matter. The touch of their hands said everything.

Chapter Six

Present Day

LEOPOLD FELT the sting across his cheek, his heart shattering with the impact.

He hadn't expected to see her at the bar. *Skye Porter*. The woman who'd stolen his heart—and whose heart he'd so recklessly broken.

For that matter, he hadn't intended to go to The Fix at all—too many bittersweet memories. But he was staying in the LBJ Presidential Suite at Austin's famous Driskill Hotel, and his corner balcony had a view of Sixth Street. He'd been in town for less than an hour, but once he'd caught a glimpse of the street and the bar … well, how could he not at least step inside and see if the place had changed?

Jürgen had pulled open the door, Leopold had stepped through, and joy had flooded him, the emotion so intense it almost knocked him backward.

It hadn't, of course. Instead, her slap had done that.

Immediately, Karl and Fritz, two of Jürgen's best bodyguards, stomped forward. Jürgen held up a hand, easing them to heel. With every eye in the place glued on him, Leopold moved closer to Skye, who'd backed away, eyes wide with shock, before the sting on his cheek had even dimmed.

He wore jeans and a black tee, as did the men who accompanied him, and Leo hoped that none of the patrons were such avid royal-watchers that they recognized him. He would hate to see Skye plastered across social media.

As he approached, she crossed her arms protectively across her chest. Her brown eyes shot daggers, though, telegraphing that she didn't regret the slap at all.

Why would she?

He dipped his head in apology, then met her eyes. "Skye."

"Don't … don't say …" She closed her eyes and he watched as she worked to control her breathing, his heart aching for her as she struggled with the words. When she opened her eyes again, the pain he saw there cut straight through his soul. "Don't you dare say you're sorry."

"But I am."

Her shoulders shook. "You're an ass and a liar and you … you used me."

"No, I—" But he cut himself off. Maybe she was right. Maybe he had.

"You made me into one of those women you…" She trailed off as if she couldn't even voice the words, then she shook her head violently. "It doesn't … matter."

He glanced around the room. There were eyes on them, but that seemed to be more about the lovers' quarrel than because they recognized him. He stepped toward her, his hand going to her upper arm before she shook it away. "Please, Skye. If we could just talk."

She lifted her chin, looking sophisticated and in control. He knew she was a lawyer now, and she looked the part. Her gaze steady. Her chin firm. Her hair was longer and hung in waves to just past her shoulders. She projected sophistication and confidence, and he couldn't be prouder.

But he couldn't tell her that. Not unless he wanted her to slap the shit out of him again.

He started to speak, intending to once again ask her to give him just a few moments of time. But she got there first.

"I don't know what you're doing back in Austin, but do me a favor and stay far away from me. In case you're confused, I'm not one of the party girls you hang with at all those villas across Europe."

Her words came out slow and he knew she was working hard to speak as clearly as possible.

He almost smiled. At least she thought he was worth the effort. For whatever cold comfort that might provide…

"Skye, please. If we could just—"

"I'm leaving now." She pushed past him and out the door, leaving the familiar scent of lavender in her wake.

God help him, he wanted to cry. Right then, he wanted to sink to the floor and bawl like a baby simply from the horrible pain of knowing how deeply he'd hurt her.

Most of all, he wanted to go after her. To explain. Hell, to grovel.

He almost did, but Jürgen stopped him. "There's no point. Why hurt her more?"

"Dammit, Jürgen, I need to—"

"*You pathetic son-of-a-bitch.*"

He turned to see a familiar blonde standing where Skye had been. "Hannah. I—"

"Fuck you, *Your Highness.*" To her credit, she kept her voice low enough that it was meant only for him. "Although I suppose I should thank you on her behalf," Hannah continued. "I mean, she learned a valuable lesson. Guess a girl like Skye wasn't video-and-sound ready enough for a guy like you to have around."

"No, I—"

"Prick."

She paused as if waiting for him to defend himself. But how could he? He hadn't left because of her speech. He hadn't left because he didn't want her. But he *had* left without saying goodbye, and in doing so, he'd hurt her. And that really did make him a prick.

"She fell in love with you." Hannah's voice was softer, the words pushed out with emotion. "Being with you … honestly, it was the first time since I've known her that she stopped being so aware of how she sounded. To her, it must have been like living in a fairy tale." She drew a deep breath and shook her head. "You might be a prince, Leo, but you're no Prince Charming."

"I never intended to hurt her."

"Well, gee. You managed without even trying. Guess that makes you special."

"No," he said. "It only makes me sad."

Chapter Seven

"GOOD MORNING, SKYE." Emily, Skye's paralegal of the last year, looked up from her computer and smiled. "Sorry to start your morning with a bang, but Mr. Porter wants to see you."

Skye's shoulders slumped and she let her leather tote slide to the floor. "Did he say what it was about?" Maybe Emily had managed to glean a clue. Nothing on her caseload was with her dad, and he was diligent about not mixing personal with business. Which meant he was about to pile another case onto her already loaded docket.

The petite redhead shook her head. "Sorry. I tried. But you know how he is."

"Did he say when?"

"As soon as you get in," she said. "So I'd say now?"

Skye sighed and nodded. "I'll just drop my …

things off in my chair and head on over to see him."

"I'll buzz Mary and let her know you're on the way," Emily said, referring to her father's assistant.

Skye stepped into her office, dropped her tote on her guest chair, and walked to the windows. She had one of the nicer views, and could see all the way down Congress Avenue to the Capitol beyond. It wasn't even nine yet, and she hadn't had nearly enough coffee for a meeting with her father. But she also knew that she couldn't delay. Tarlton Porter was a man who waited for no one, including his daughter. Now that Mary knew she was in the office, she'd be getting pinged if she wasn't there in the next two minutes.

Getting pinged by Tarlton Porter was every associate's worst nightmare. And his daughter was no exception.

Resigned, she drew a deep breath, then headed into the carpeted hallway. Her father's office was two floors above, so she took the back exit by the ladies' room, and entered the stairwell. She didn't get nearly enough exercise as it was, so she tried to take the stairs whenever possible. It also lessened the chances that she would run into someone in the elevator and feel compelled to make small talk. If there was one thing Skye hated, it was small talk. She didn't want to speak, but assumed people would think she was rude if she didn't. But what should she say? Especially when she knew that half the people she was supposedly chatting with were only nodding politely and couldn't understand half of what she was saying.

She exited the stairwell on the twentieth floor, used her key card to get back in through the rear entrance, and followed the lushly carpeted perimeter hallway to her father's massive corner office. Mary looked up as she approached, her smile bright. "That was quick."

Skye shrugged. "I was aiming for brownie … points. Do you think I earned any?"

Mary laughed. "With your father? Brownies are hard to come by."

Wasn't that the case?

"Do you know what he wants? Is it about the symposium?"

"Honestly, I don't. I dropped my car at the shop this morning and arrived after your father. All he said was that I should buzz you to come see him. Sorry."

"No problem." Skye appreciated the poking around that Mary did for all the associates, trying to give the younger attorneys a heads-up. But she couldn't expect Mary to be able to do that every time. "So I should go on in?"

Mary glanced down at her phone and nodded. "He's not on a call. I'll let him know you're coming." She pressed the intercom button. "Skye's here, sir," she said, as Skye walked forward and pushed the door open. Her father paced behind his desk, dictating what sounded like a letter about a trademark issue with one of the firm's international clients.

He saw her, lifted a finger, and didn't even stumble on his sentence. Skye took a seat in one of the guest chairs, grateful for the extra time to gather herself.

At fifty-eight, her father was still an incredibly attractive man, with salt-and-pepper hair and a confident demeanor that seemed reflected in the hard lines of his face. A brilliant attorney, he took no shit from anyone, but also praised good work and encouraged young attorneys to try new arguments and to never simply go with whatever approach to a case that he suggested. It was only when an associate cut corners or sank under the weight of their workload or the firm's expectations that his temper showed—and it was a hell of a temper.

Tarlton Porter was one of the best attorneys that Skye had ever had the pleasure of working with, and she appreciated the fact that he didn't give her special treatment. He pushed her to do better, which she liked. But he also wanted to see her career grow to the same heights as his. And in the appellate world, that meant getting a reputation as the kind of attorney who could eventually argue a case before the United States Supreme Court.

That wasn't something Skye wanted for herself. But she knew that her father did. And she wondered what path he was going to try to push her toward today.

"That's all, Mary," he said into the recording, then turned seamlessly toward Skye. "Hello, sweetheart."

"What's up, Daddy?" Unprofessional, maybe, but a habit she hadn't been able to break unless clients were around.

"How are you coming on planning your talk for the symposium?"

Skye frowned, certain he hadn't called her in there just for that. The symposium was still two weeks away. Still, since he brought it up...

"I've made … some notes," she said, forcing herself to speak slowly. He might be her father, but he was still intimidating, and that tightness in her gut translated to a tightness in her speech as well. It was damn frustrating, especially since she knew that her speech was what her father so desperately wanted to fix about her. And despite visiting as many speech therapists as she had, he continued to hold onto the hope that she could conquer the dysarthria with nothing more than brutal willpower. Which, of course, was why he was insisting she speak to hundreds of key clients and potentials.

It had to stop. She swallowed, then stood, wanting to be at the same level as her father. "But … honestly, I wanted to … talk to you … about it."

He father sat behind his desk and leaned back, his hands under his chin, forefingers steepled. "Oh?"

Skye cleared her throat and remained standing, keeping her feet planted and her hands by her sides. Her father was very attuned to any signs of nervousness, and he considered them weaknesses. When he caught associates squirming and shifting, there were always consequences. His theory was if they acted nervous in front of him, how would they act in front of opposing counsel? Give something away through nerves, and you might end up screwing a client.

"Having me … speak is a … mistake. You're trying to … gain new clients for … our international law practice. But … Daddy, I don't …practice international law. I do appellate work. So … having me present this paper is … ridiculous."

"I don't disagree with your assessment, sweetheart," he said, as waves of relief flooded through her. "But I think you're looking at this all wrong."

The relief turned to ice, and she froze. "Am I?"

"You wrote an incredible paper on agnatic primogeniture, and its role in the international community, particularly with regard to countries working to amend their constitutions to change that particular mode of succession."

"I know what I wrote." She stiffened as she spoke. It had been an odd topic for her law review article her final year of law school, but under the circumstances she'd been extremely interested in the subject. Now, of course, she regretted it.

First, Leo had broken her heart, and writing the article hadn't been the balm she'd hoped. Worse, she'd been reminded of him every day that she was researching and writing. And those were a lot of days.

Now, she had a second basis for regret. Because apparently that paper was the lever her father needed to put her front and center so that she could —according to his plan anyway—just get over it.

Considering all that, she should've slapped Leo's face even harder last night.

Her father remained silent, and she squirmed. She knew this was a mind game, forcing her to speak, and though she didn't want to give in, the words came anyway. "Daddy, I don't … practice that. It was … just for law … review."

"And that law review article was extensively published and received numerous awards and accolades."

"But it's not what we do."

"Maybe it should be."

"Oh." She sat down, then drew a breath. "Well,

it's not … what I do. Appellate law, remember? You can … share the article, but I … don't need to speak." *Dial it in, Skye.* She was having trouble controlling her breathing. Just the thought of standing on that stage—of speaking to all those people—it was both mortifying and terrifying.

She straightened her shoulders and put all her effort into slowing down and breathing properly. "Even if … the firm expands the international group, I … won't be involved. So … why speak? It's not … like that … article will rake in … clients."

"One day, you will very likely be a partner in this firm, and you will be involved even if it's not your practice area. On top of that, you're wrong."

She shook her head, confused. "Wrong?"

"I know you thought that it was ridiculous to add you to the symposium agenda, but we actually do have a potential new client because of that article and the promise of your participation in the symposium."

"Oh." She sat back, thrown off about that revelation.

"Come meet him." He tapped a few keys on his computer, then turned his attention back to her.

"What? Now?"

"He's just arrived. Douglas is with him," he added, referring to one of the other partners.

"Well, then you hardly need me." How could her father be so dense? She was not an asset where bringing in clients was concerned. Not by a long shot.

"Skye, the man specifically referenced your article. There is no way that Douglas and I are going to conduct this meeting without having you present. I'm not asking you as my daughter, I'm telling you as your boss."

"Right. Fine. Whatever."

She watched as his face softened. "Sweetheart, you wrote an excellent article. You are expected at the meeting. And you will do fine."

She stood, looking down at the floor. "If you say so," she said, but she didn't believe it at all.

Skye followed her father to the elevator, then up the two stories to the twenty-second floor, which the firm had devoted to conference space and the firm's law library. Eight conference rooms dotted the perimeter, offering multiple views of the Austin area. The library and a small refreshment area took up the middle, and as they passed an open doorway, she waved to a few associates who were highlighting briefs and reading case law at the long, wooden library tables.

Since they were meeting only one client, she expected her father would lead her to one of the smaller rooms. Instead, he headed toward the corner conference room with stunning views of both downtown and the river.

The floor's conference rooms were set up so that the only windows were on the exterior walls, providing complete privacy for what was happening within, and Skye assumed that the client had come with an entourage. What other reason could justify using the largest venue?

As she followed her father, Skye's nerves started to flutter as they always did before she talked to a stranger. Honestly, maybe she'd made the wrong career decision, after all. Maybe she needed to get an IT job where she could sit behind a computer and not have to talk to a human at all.

Or maybe she should try her hand at writing a legal thriller. Only if it took off, she'd end up doing book signings and book tours where she'd be expected to speak to fans. That sounded terrifying.

Honestly, the truth was that she already had the perfect job, and one that she loved when it worked the way it was supposed to. What she needed was a different father, who didn't shove her through doors and expect her to become Eliza Doolittle, suddenly polished and proper and speaking beautifully.

She half smiled at the thought. She knew her father loved her and wanted the best career for her. The trouble was that their ideas of *best* were so disparate. And though he loved her, he didn't hesitate to push her into situations where she was required to speak.

He thought she would undergo some magical transformation that would let him shed his guilt. She knew that nothing would change, and the clients and colleagues would struggle to understand her slurred and slow speech until, finally, they became accustomed to the cadence and flow and no longer looked at her with pity in their eyes.

That, of course, was the worst. The pity. Or, even more mortifying, that glint that suggested she wasn't intelligent. That somehow her stumbling speech reflected a stumbling mind as well. She knew it wasn't true. Her friends knew it wasn't true, so why the hell did she care what strangers thought? She shouldn't. But she did.

It was slightly better now. Her pedigree as a lawyer granted her some modicum of respect and the benefit of the doubt. But when she'd been in school...

She shuddered. Those had been hard times.

Her father paused outside the conference room door. "This is an important client," he said, his voice low, even though they both knew that sound did not travel through those walls. "I'm not telling you that to make you nervous, but to understand that your paper has drawn interest from unusual and important places."

"Okay."

Skye wondered who the client could possibly be. It wasn't as if there were that many people interested in the line of royal succession in countries across the globe. Then again, the paper covered the process of amending a country's constitution or legislative process, and those concepts could be applied more broadly. So perhaps it made sense that potential international clients wanted to learn more.

Still, though, it seemed odd that her paper was the catalyst.

Her father pushed open the door, and she fell in step behind him, making sure she had a smile on her face and an interested and engaged gleam in her eye.

She thrust out her hand automatically, her mind so full of questions that she wasn't really looking at who might be in the room. Then her father stepped aside, and she got a full view of the man rising from the chair at the head of the table.

It was Leo.

Chapter Eight

SKYE FROZE, and for the first time she understood the expression *deer in the headlights*.

"Ms. Porter," Leo said, stepping toward her with his hand extended. "It's a pleasure to meet you."

He took her hand before she had a chance to either pull it away or melt into the floor. And—damn him to hell—she felt that familiar tingle. A sensual awareness that used to make her deliriously happy.

Right now, it just pissed her off. She withdrew her hand, careful to keep her face unreadable. She could only hope that she was succeeding. "You as well, Mr.—?"

Her father stepped forward, practically bursting with glee. "Skye, I'd like you to meet His Royal

Highness, Prince Stephan Leopold of Avelle-am-see."

Skye swallowed, feeling like she was lost in some nightmare. Or an alternate universe. "What are you doing here?"

Her father stiffened, looking at her with utter shock. And no wonder.

"Skye," Douglas Crane said, his expression stern. "The prince is here to discuss international law."

She should keep her mouth shut—she knew that—but emotion had taken over, and apparently she'd forgotten how to exercise control. "Why?" she demanded, looking between the two men.

"I'm attending the symposium," Leo said, his eyes locking on hers. "And I'm intrigued by your firm's expertise."

"The prince read your article," her father said, a question in his eye and a hint of anger in his voice.

Not surprising. It wasn't every day that royal clients came to a firm in Austin, Texas. But she knew damn well this wasn't about the work the firm did. This was about her.

She opened her mouth, unsure of what she was going to say, but certain it wasn't going to be words that would make her father happy.

Leo took a step forward, diving in before Skye

could manage a word. "Perhaps I could speak to Ms. Porter alone?"

Her eyes went wide, and she started to shake her head. Her father responded first, though, and while she'd expected him to back up her refusal—why would he or Douglas want her alone with this man when she'd already been rude and off-putting?—he surprised her by dipping his head in acquiescence and saying, "Of course, Your Highness."

"But … I—"

"I'll be in my office," her father said, entirely ignoring her discomfort and predicament.

"Buzz us if you need anything at all," Douglas added, his expression stern but polite.

Her father hesitated in the doorway. "Skye, I know you will treat His Highness with the respect he deserves."

Right-o. That would be exactly none.

But she didn't say that. Instead, she nodded, then gave her father and his partner a weak and watery smile that was all she could manage. Then she stood still until the door clicked shut behind them. Only then did she explode.

"*Respect*? Why. Are. You. Here?" For once, her words were clear. Each word forced out like a shot from a gun. She was alight with fury. And Leo—damn him—didn't seem affected at all.

"Exactly what your father said. I'm looking for legal advice."

"I … don't believe you."

He winced, and shook his head. "I read your law review article, Skye. I want to work with you."

She shook her head. "I don't do international law, and I certainly don't work for you. I think you need to leave."

She felt lightheaded, and she walked to the chair at the head of the table hoping he couldn't tell how rubbery her legs had become. She pulled it out, then sat down, her hands clasped in front of her. "This isn't going … to happen."

He moved down the table, sitting in the chair to her immediate left around the oval conference table. He angled his chair so that he was facing her. For a moment their eyes met, and she thought she saw regret in those deep blue eyes. Then they went flat, the face of someone used to hiding his emotions.

She glanced down at the table, not wanting to look at him. "You broke my heart."

"I know. I'm sorry. That's another reason I'm here today—to apologize to you."

She shot him a glare. "Seriously? After all this time?" She had no idea what emotion she was feeling. Anger, hurt, rage, confusion? It was all too much of a mess. And the worst part? Some tiny, traitorous part of her was giddy about seeing him again.

But Skye wasn't stupid. She knew perfectly well that if she spent any time with this man, she would get hurt all over again. And it had taken so long for her to get over him the first time.

She faced him, then focused on her speech, purposefully ignoring those dangerously hypnotic eyes. "I'm sure you'll find … another firm. Try Washington. We have an office there full of international law experts. In London and Brussels, too. I'm … sure anyone at those offices could help you."

"You're saying that you won't work with me on this?"

"I'm saying you need to leave." She pushed back from the table and walked to the door, ready to pull it open. "Don't feel obligated to say goodbye. You … didn't the last time."

"Your father will be disappointed."

"Is that a threat?"

"Of course not. I'm only pointing out that your father seemed excited by the idea of having a prince for a client, even one who wants to keep a low profile while he's in Austin."

"You want to … guilt me into taking … this assignment? Hire the firm if you want. But you … won't be working with … me."

She turned the knob, her heart pounding painfully. She had to get out before the tears started to flow.

"Skye, the entire reason I am sitting here right now is because of that article you wrote."

She shook her head. She should pull open the door and bolt, but somehow, she was frozen to the spot, her body hot, her pulse pounding, her head humming.

Was this a panic attack? This might be a panic attack.

When they were together in the past, she'd always been so at ease. Those had been the best days of her life. She hadn't worried about what he thought or the way she sounded. But she was worrying about it now.

Because she wanted him to hear very clearly how much she wanted him gone.

Bolstering her courage, she drew in a breath and turned back to meet his eyes dead on. She forced herself to speak slowly even though she wanted to blurt out the words. She wanted him to understand every damn syllable. The words came in bursts and slightly slurred. But at least they came.

"My father is ambitious for me. But once I tell him that you're a lying man-whore who used and dumped me, I promise he will kick you out of this office and get the press involved. Whatever low-key visit to Austin that you wanted will be shot in the foot right then."

"You wouldn't do that."

"Try me. He doesn't know about us. Nobody does. I never told anybody that I dated a prince who used me, and I ripped that stupid picture of you off the board at The Fix. I erased you, Leo. Scrubbed you from my life."

"Did you?" His voice was oddly gentle. "Is that why you wrote that law review article? Because you'd put me behind you?"

Ice cold anger burned inside her, along with mortification that he saw her so clearly. "I will tell my father and the press everything if that's what it takes to get you out of this office."

He took a step toward her. She put a hand up, tilting her head and glaring at him. He froze.

"Skye—"

"Just go."

"What will you tell your father? He's going to wonder why I walked out of here."

"I'll just tell him the truth. That you realized I wasn't even close to good enough for you, and so you decided to just walk away."

Chapter Nine

Two Years Ago

"LEO!"

Skye's voice hit him the moment he and Jürgen stepped through the door at The Fix on Sixth. He searched the room, quickly finding her by the dartboard with Hannah and Griffin. She grinned and waved. Best of all, she didn't appear the least bit self-conscious about shouting his name.

He blew her a kiss and pointed to a booth. She nodded, then hugged her friends before hurrying toward him while Jürgen—an excellent bodyguard and an even better friend—made himself scarce.

As she got closer, her smile widened, her brown eyes glittering with joy as she threw herself into his arms, her legs locking around his upper thighs so that he was forced to palm her ass to hold her up. Which wasn't a bad thing at all.

"Guess what?"

"I'm going out on a limb and saying that it's good news."

"They posted grades." She spoke slowly, her breathing steady despite her obvious excitement. "Now guess which girl got all A's—including the high-A in antitrust law."

"Um, Ellie?" Skye's law school bestie was a charming woman, but she was also barely skating by.

"She managed a C-minus, and she's thrilled."

He bounced her in his arms. "Then I'm guessing you're the girl who got all A's."

She nodded happily. "And I managed that despite … spending far too much time with this cute guy I've … been hanging around with."

"Perhaps that guy is your good luck charm."

She leaned forward and kissed him, soft and sweet. "Maybe he is."

"I'm thrilled for you. But not at all surprised. I know how hard you've been studying." He'd been there beside her for each study session, poring over his own physics notes and annotating the results of various simulations he and Professor Malkin were running. They'd both worked hard—with some quite delicious study breaks to make the time pass faster.

Still in his embrace, she nodded over her shoulder toward Griffin and Hannah. "Just to make sure my ego … didn't get out of control, they were kicking my ass at darts."

He gave her butt a squeeze. "I can think of things to do with your ass, but kicking isn't one of them."

She leaned forward, kissed him, then playfully bit his lower lip, tugging on it just enough that he felt the heat curl all the way down to his cock, until he had no choice but to put her down or risk entirely inappropriate behavior right there in the bar.

He loosened his grip, and she slid down his body, the motion doing such incredible things to him, it took all his effort not to moan. She made him feel things he'd never felt before. Arousal, sure. But something deeper. More intense. More meaningful.

He craved her more than he'd ever craved any woman, and he'd waited longer for her than he had for any woman. He knew he'd fallen hard and fast, but it felt real. It felt right. And although that was undeniably odd, he couldn't deny that he liked it.

And honestly, why should he deny it? Quantum entanglement was real enough, he knew that without a doubt. The phenomenon of paired particles reacting and responding to one another even when they were separated by great distance. It applied to people, too. Because damned if he wasn't certain that Skye had been there all along, his paired particle.

"I like that," she'd said when he'd told her as much during a study break. "I think it's the perfect metaphor … for us."

He knew she didn't understand the physics of it, but she understood the core. He'd kissed her then, long and hard and deep. She'd moaned, her mouth against his, then she'd boldly pulled off her shirt, and he'd almost died on the spot. She was perfect. Her breasts spilling out over the top of her bra, her pale skin begging to be kissed.

He'd unfastened the front clasp, then tasted her nipple, sucking on it as she made the kind of whimpering sounds that drove him absolutely crazy.

He wanted more, and he'd kissed his way down her body, his tongue teasing her navel, his teeth tugging at the button on her jeans, then moving lower and lower until…

Except they hadn't gotten to *until.*

She'd stopped him, telling him she wanted to, but that she was still a virgin and thought it better to wait until after finals. Especially since her antitrust class was kicking her ass.

"I'm sorry."

"No," he'd told her, kissing her gently. "I like having something to look forward to."

That had led to three full weeks of wild desire

topped off by a permanent ache in his cock that became his new normal.

It had also led to some soul-searching and guilt. Because how the hell could he be her first when he knew nothing could come of it? As the heir to the throne, he would be expected to marry, yes. But his choices for a bride were limited. And American lawyers were not within those parameters.

The bottom line was that whatever was between them couldn't last. The most they could have was a Texas fling, and while he'd had many a fling with many a woman, Skye deserved more.

He didn't want just sex with Skye. He wanted romance. He wanted passion. He wanted a connection.

Most of all, he wanted her. And there was no way that he could have her.

An hour later, his melancholy had passed, replaced by the laughter and teasing that came with drinking beer while playing darts with her, Hannah, and Griffin.

They were about to take a break and order another round when Skye tugged him sideways. He stopped, looking quizzically back at her. After a moment, she cleared her throat and gently tugged her hand away. He mourned the loss of contact, but at the same time, he was grateful for it. More and more often, he was finding it hard to let her go.

She cleared her throat. "There's something I want you to do. It will be a total blast."

"Oh no. What are you dragging me into?"

She gave his hand a tug. "Just come with me," she urged. He didn't protest. Right then, he was certain he would follow her forever.

But when she led him to the far wall, he felt his trepidation rising. He knew exactly what she was about to ask, and he started to shake his head. "Oh no. No, no, no."

"Please." She grinned at him and batted her eyes, exaggerating every movement until he had to laugh.

"I don't want to be on the board," he protested.

"But you would put everybody else to shame. Seriously, you're like some Hollywood star."

"Thank you for trying to butter me up, but no."

Leopold had learned that, not long ago, The Fix on Sixth held a Man of the Month calendar contest in order to raise money to save the bar. Leopold didn't know the whole story, but obviously the bar had been saved. And since then, the bar had started a ritual of taking posed pics of willing customers and tacking them up on a poster-sized calendar. One for every day.

It had become a thing at the bar. Unlike the calendar, the men weren't shirtless and the pictures weren't published anywhere. But sometimes customers photographed the board and shared the candid photos all across social media. For that reason, #TheFixOnSixth was conveniently displayed over the image board.

It was, on the whole, a great promotional strategy for the bar, and while Leopold respected that, he did not want to participate. What if some royal-watching customer came over to check out the board? What a ridiculous way to have his cover blown.

Except there was Skye doing puppy dog eyes at him with so much exaggeration that he had to laugh.

"Oh, come on, Leo. It will be fun. Don't you want to memorialize this month?"

"Desperately," he said, making her laugh from the leer in his voice.

"Okay, disappoint me." She exhaled an exaggerated sigh. "It's not like I won't judge … you for the rest of eternity … for this moment."

Now, he really was laughing. This woman matched him so perfectly, their senses of humor lining up like a covalent bond. Or back to quantum entanglement.

He saw Tyree approaching with a camera, and knew that he was sunk. Besides, he'd already conceded in his head. As far as he was concerned, what Skye wanted Skye got, and she obviously wanted him to do this silly thing.

"Hey, Leo." Tyree reached out for a high-five, his large hand practically swallowing Leopold's. He lifted the camera. "Are you going to be joining our calendar board today?"

Leopold put on his best smile even as he watched Jürgen scowling at him from across the room. "I guess I am," he said.

A few minutes later, he had a copy of the photo that Tyree had selected from the dozen or so snaps he'd taken.

"I love it," Skye said, pulling it off the photo printer. "Can I keep it?"

"What? My first cover shoot and you're taking the evidence?"

She pressed it against her heart, and when she said, "Please," it didn't feel like teasing.

"Yes," he said softly. "Of course, you can."

"Thank you." She hesitated a moment, then held it out to him. "Will you sign it?"

Wasn't *that* an inconvenient question?

"Great big famous cover model that you are, I want to get a piece of that." She added a leer to her voice that made him laugh.

"Do you?"

She looked him slowly up and down, making every atom in his body accelerate its spin. "Yeah," she said, her voice low and a little shy. "I really do."

"Skye..." He didn't know what to say. He saw the want in her eyes; he heard it in her voice. And oh, but he wanted it, too.

He held out his hand. "Let me have the picture."

She did, and he borrowed a Sharpie from one of the passing servers. He wrote the first thing he thought of—*Love, Leo*—then passed it back to her.

He watched as she read it, her hands trembling slightly. Her teeth grazed her lower lip, and she looked up at him through lowered lashes. Then she rose up on her toes and kissed his cheek, and he felt like nothing he could do as king could feel better than this.

"Thank you."

"Anything to make you happy." As he spoke, he realized just how true that was. For no reason other than to make her happy, he'd just shared a part of himself with the world. Not that he expected the photo to get out, but there was a bit of a risk, and he'd taken it for her. He was tumbling off into space, and he knew it.

The weird thing was, he loved it.

They ordered another round of drinks, then sipped their Loaded Coronas. He told her how the research with Professor Malkin was going, and she asked all the right questions. Then he listened as she talked about her summer job at her father's firm and the federal clerkship she hoped to get after graduation. A one-year term on the Second Circuit in New York, after which she'd return home to Austin and the family business.

At one point, he realized that he hadn't even noticed the slur in her words or the pauses in her sentences.

"No desire to see what other firm might want you?" he asked. "Or to do something entirely different? Teach or go in-house?"

She shook her head. "That firm is home. I practically grew up there. By the time I was twelve, I was actually proofreading briefs. By the time I was fifteen, I was writing them. It's not a lack of ambition or me being stuck in a rut. It's wanting to help continue building something excellent that started generations ago."

He nodded. "I get that. I've worked in my father's business all my life as well. And I've pretty much learned how to run it. Fortunately, I don't have to yet, but I could if something happened to him."

"Do you want to?"

"Run the business?" He shook his head. "No. My sister would be much better at that. My passion is physics."

She nodded. "I can hear how much you love it when you talk about it."

"I do. But the business is important to the family, and there are reasons why my sister can't take over. So I'm afraid it may fall to me. No, not afraid. I know that it will."

Her forehead wrinkled, and she frowned. "I'm sorry. Maybe you could—"

"No. Thanks, but I'd rather not talk about it. Believe me, I've spent much of my life wondering how to avoid it. It's not a fun subject. I'd rather talk about, well, anything else."

"Fair enough. How about the moon landing? I mean, Neil Armstrong. What a guy, right?"

He practically exploded with laughter. "Yes. The moon landing, and then we can move on to old James Bond films."

The weird thing was they did exactly that. They talked about the moon landing and the current state of space exploration. They talked about the law, then physics. From there, they somehow managed to move on to Blumhouse horror movies and twist that over to James Bond, with both agreeing that Sean Connery was the best.

They bounced from topic to topic with such seamless ease, it was almost as if they were characters in a play who had rehearsed this conversation over and over again. Or a couple who had been together for years and not just weeks.

Quantum entanglement, he thought again.

It was unexpected. It was wonderful.

And it was so damned inconvenient.

They finally moved their conversation from the

bar to the street, then walked back to her place. He paid no attention to their surroundings. He was too wrapped up in the conversation and the feel of her hand twined with his.

Foolish, yes, but Jürgen was out there somewhere, making sure all was well. It was a lack of privacy, true. But one Leo grew up with, and it was so familiar that he barely thought about his constant shadow.

It was past midnight when they reached the door to her condo, and he expected her to invite him in. They'd have a drink, talk a bit more. He'd hold her, kiss her, lose himself in her. But that was as far as it would go, and after a few hours, he'd leave, summon Jürgen, and head back to their rented house.

Tonight, though, she paused after punching in the entry code.

"I have one condition tonight," she said, her eyes locked on his. "If you come in, you don't leave until morning."

He felt the shift in the air as the universe aligned. "Skye, you—we—you know I won't be staying in America. I can't promise you—"

"I don't care." She slid into his arms. "I'm falling for you, Leo. And maybe I can't have you forever. But if you let me, I can have you for now. Please," she added in a whisper. "I trust you. More than that I want you to be my first."

He should walk away. He shouldn't claim this moment as his own when he held onto so many secrets.

He should tell her no, but he didn't. Because he was a selfish ass, and oh, God, how he craved her. Yes, he'd have to go back home, but it wouldn't be tomorrow or even next week.

They had time, and he wanted to fill it with Skye.

Chapter Ten

Present Day

"SO YOU SAID NO?" Hannah sat across from her at one of the tables at The Fix. "To working with a prince?" She shot a sideways glance at Bart, Skye's roommate, and lifted her brows before turning her attention back to Skye. "Do you really think that was a good idea?"

"Of course it was," Bart said. He reached across the table and squeezed Skye's hand. "The guy was a son of a bitch."

Skye squeezed back. Bart hadn't been around two years ago when everything had fallen apart with Leo, when his abrupt disappearance the morning after the first and only time they'd made love had shattered her dreams. But he was one of her closest friends now, and he knew the story. And, yeah, she appreciated the loyalty.

She cocked her head, looking at Hannah. Hannah was one of her closest friends too. And while she wished that Hannah was on her and Bart's side, she couldn't deny that she had to at least give what her friend said a little consideration.

"I know that from a career standpoint, it was probably an idiot move. But his leaving destroyed me. How am I supposed to do that again?"

"It's been two years," Hannah said. "And everything's changed now. And don't forget—*he* was the asshole, but you got screwed. This is a chance to fix that, because if you bring him on as a client, at least you're getting something from him." She shrugged. "Even if it's only massive billable hours and clout for the firm."

Everything had changed? Skye supposed it had. Everything that mattered, anyway. Before, she'd allowed herself the fantasy that they would end up together. Now that she knew who and what he was, she knew that she'd dodged a bullet.

Even if he'd wanted her in his homeland, she couldn't do it. Being that much in the public eye? It would be a nightmare.

More important, he'd never asked. He'd done the opposite of asking. He bolted back home without even saying goodbye.

She'd been despondent at first, her whole body

aching with waves of alternating grief and anger. But then someone had recognized him from the picture at The Fix.

At first, Skye had thought they were just bull-shitting her. Then she'd done some research. And, sure enough, he was a prince. A prince who'd left the States to go to the side of his ailing father, the king, who had not been expected to live through the week.

The king had pulled through, and though Skye kept expecting Leo to call or come back to Texas, even if just to see Professor Malkin, he never did. And though the hurt never fully went away, it did fade. After all, the hurt was only about her ego.

The real truth was that he'd done her a favor. She couldn't even imagine what it would be like to date a royal, even one from a relatively anonymous country. There would be press. She would be expected to make statements.

She'd never taken anxiety drugs, but she had a feeling that a life on Leo's arm would require intra-venous Xanax. No, that definitely wasn't happening.

Which, of course, meant that Hannah was right. Things *had* changed. Everything except the way she felt about him.

She reached for her wine and took a sip to hide what was undoubtedly showing on her face, because in the conference room, she'd felt those butterflies again. That warm and wonderful feeling that she'd felt the first time she met him. And she wasn't sure if she could work with him on a professional level unless those butterflies were exterminated.

"If you don't face him," Hannah said gently, "It's never going to go away."

Skye sighed. "How do you do that?"

Hannah shrugged and grinned. "You're my best friend. I can read you like a book. That and the fact that you've told me you'd never gotten over him. But you know why, don't you?"

Skye rolled her eyes, not wanting to say the answer out loud.

Bart looked between the two of them. "So you're suggesting that she work with this guy so that she can be close to this guy so she can get over this guy? That's the most ridiculous thing I've ever heard."

"No," Skye said. "I actually think it's pretty smart." She could hear the misery in her voice. Being close to him wouldn't be easy. But if they were working on a professional level then once he left, *that* would be the relationship that lingered. Not the long nights in his arms and gentle kisses. Instead it would be document revisions and strategy sessions for how to approach his advisors. Hardly romantic stuff.

"But it's not only about getting over him," Hannah said.

"I know. I know," Skye said. "It's important to my dad."

Hannah rolled her eyes. "To your dad? It should be important to you, too. You know that, Skye. He would be a hell of a client, and all of the branches of the firm are going to know that you're the reason he came. Because of that article you wrote. This is a way to make absolutely clear that you belong at a firm as important as Porter, Jenson & Kaye no matter what your last name is."

"Okay, I changed my mind," Bart said. "Hannah really does have a point. I mean, landing a royal as a client for my firm? The partners would go wild. Hell, they'd give *me* a crown."

Skye couldn't help a grin at the mental image of Bart wearing a crown. He was one hell of a good-looking man, but it was Leo that she was picturing in the royal attire.

Mentally, she waved the image away. She did not need him in her head dressed as a royal or just dressed as Leo. Either way, it wasn't a good idea.

"He's in town through the symposium," Bart said, looking up from his phone. "It says here that the prince is going to New York after that for some meetings at the UN. But that's a full two weeks you have to work with him. And get him out of your system."

She pressed her fingertips to her temple. "Two years ago, I would have been thrilled to have him in the audience. Now, it just … makes me even more nervous." She shuddered. "At least my stage fright is winning out over my angst about Leo."

Hannah reached over and put her hand on Skye's in a sympathetic gesture. Bart just frowned, his finger tapping on the tabletop.

"What?" Skye asked.

"You're nervous because you're speaking in front of a crowd," Bart said.

"Thank you for stating the obvious," Skye said.

He stared at her, then twirled his hand in a *come on* gesture. She shrugged, clueless.

He sighed with exasperation. "Skye, have you ever taken a public speaking class?"

She gaped at him. "Uh, no. I thought I would … save the world the torture of having to listen to me speak publicly. Not to mention … terrifying."

"And yet you're doing it at symposium."

"Thank you for playing on my worst fears when I'm trying to have a drink."

"I'm just saying that maybe a little training wouldn't be a bad idea. And considering how many public speeches a prince makes, perhaps it would be a good idea to ask Leo to help you get ready."

Hannah sat up straighter. "Oh, yes. You're already going to be spending time with him doing the work on succession, right? So maybe you should get something in exchange other than billable hours."

"I don't know what you two are—*oh.*" She looked between the two of them then grinned.

"It's the perfect idea," Bart said. "You know I'm right."

Skye sat back unable to fight a small smile. It was the perfect idea.

She only hoped it wasn't also a perfect mistake.

Chapter Eleven

SKYE FELT ONLY SLIGHTLY guilty about calling Emily at home on a Friday night, but she wanted to contact Leo right then while she was still slightly buzzed from drinks with Hannah and Bart. Because as soon as her head cleared, she was certain she'd lose her nerve.

Now she stood at the door to his suite, having been cleared by the guard posted at the elevator door. Two years ago, he'd lived in an apartment, and there'd been no guards, no procedures. Then again, two years ago she hadn't known he was a prince.

"*Jerk*," she muttered, but even though the word was completely accurate—even though the way he'd bolted still stung—some traitorous part deep inside her hoped that he would accept her proposal. Not because she wanted him, of course. But because Hannah and Bart were right. Who better to teach her how to be calm in front of an audience? Because unless she could control her nerves, no one would be able to understand a single word she said.

And, okay, yes. Maybe she wanted to see him, too. But only for closure.

Just do this.

Right. Okay.

She drew a breath, lifted her hand, and rapped on the door.

A moment later, it opened inward, and she found herself looking at the sharp-cut features and hard, almost-black eyes of Jürgen Braun, Leo's best friend. Except of course, he wasn't really. He was an attendant or courtier, or whatever you called someone who worked for a royal.

"Ms. Porter," Jürgen said, his accent as thick as she'd remembered. "It's a pleasure to see you again." He swept his arm to usher her in, and as she crossed the threshold she almost admonished him to call her Skye. They'd been friends, after all.

Except they hadn't. Not really. It had all been fake.

Her back was to him, and she took a moment to collect herself before glancing over her shoulder to smile politely. "It's good to see you again."

He hesitated, and for a moment she had the impression he was going to speak. Then he simply gestured for her to take a seat. "His Highness will be out soon."

"Right." Her throat went dry, and she started toward the ornate sofa. She knew the suite well, as the firm often put VIPs up there. It was smaller than she'd expect for royalty with only one bedroom and less than a thousand square feet. But it was beautifully appointed and had a view of Sixth Street from the corner balcony.

She imagined that someone from Leo's security team stayed up at night on the couch while he took the bedroom. "You're his security guard," she said to Jürgen as the pieces fell into place.

He tilted his head in acquiescence. "I've been on His Highness's security team since his thirteenth birthday. I was sixteen and following in my father's footsteps. His Highness promoted me to the office of security chief on his twenty-first birthday.

"I thought you were friends. But I guess the whole damn thing was one big show."

Jürgen's shoulders stiffened. "It is my honor to count Leopold among my closest friends." He spoke formally, his words clipped. He said nothing else, and although he met her eyes, she couldn't help but think she saw a hint of regret there.

Yeah, well, she regretted a lot, too.

"Lucky you," she said, knowing she should stay quiet. "To have such an honorable prince as your friend."

He didn't waver from his military rest pose, but his lips parted. Whether it was a reflex or he intended to say something else, she didn't know because the door to the bedroom opened, and his eyes cut that direction, his body stiffening to attention.

Skye turned, expecting Leo, only to see a petite brunette with an elfin face and cherry red lips step through the doorway, her fingers working the final button on a man's white dress shirt worn untucked over a gray pencil skirt. A leather tote hung carelessly off her shoulder.

"Thank you, Your Highness," she said, as Leo followed her out of the room, looking deliciously casual in jeans and a plain white T-shirt. "I'll see you tomorrow."

"I look forward to it." He gave the girl a quick smile, and she headed out, Jürgen following her into the hallway, presumably to escort her down the elevator, a royal walk of shame if ever there was one.

"Skye," Leo said, closing the distance between them in two long strides.

She took a step back, suddenly wishing that Jürgen was in the room, because his presence might —*might*—cool her temper.

"Re…really, Leo?" She cringed, wanting to roll into a ball right then because *this* was how she came off? Not cool and unaffected, but instead so gobsmacked that her words misbehaved even more than usual.

"Really, what?"

"I called … up. You knew … I was coming. And … this is what … I walk in on?"

His brows rose, but he said nothing.

She exhaled loudly, then shook her head. No longer even caring about how she sounded. "I guess I … dodged a bullet … when you left."

For a moment, he only studied her. Then he dipped his head. "I suppose you did." His voice was as polished as it had been in the conference room earlier that afternoon. "But if you're talking about Talia, you have no reason to be jealous."

"Jealous?" She took a step back, shaking her head. "I am so over … you. I'm just saying that I knew you were a … ridiculous playboy in your own country. But … I didn't realize you were playing that game here, too. Should I be honored to be one of your … American contingent? Me and—what was her name? Tabby Cat?"

He raised his brows and she wanted to kick herself for going too far. For letting her jealousy spew out. But, dammit, she'd been unprepared for how strong it was. For how much she'd actually missed him.

And for how much it hurt seeing him with another woman.

She'd read all the articles and seen all the

pictures, of course. For a prince who'd before kept a reasonably low profile, he'd been all over the tabloids after he'd left her, his escapades with socialites and film stars and other royals popping up so regularly in her social media that she finally just closed most of her accounts.

It had hurt, yeah. But mostly it had only reassured her that his departure was for the best. He was a player, and not the kind of man she wanted.

She knew that about him. And yet one real live glimpse of him with another woman, and she turned into a jealous girlfriend.

Except, of course, she wasn't his girlfriend.

For that matter, she never really had been. She'd simply been one in a string. Not photographed or filmed, but part of that chain nonetheless.

"How can I help you, Ms. Porter?"

His voice wasn't cold, but its formality bothered her more than it should.

No. That's good. Formal and professional.

She cleared her throat and concentrated on speaking slowly. "I changed my mind."

His brow rose. "Did you? And what exactly are we talking about?"

"My paper. You said you … wanted to work with me. How exactly?"

For a moment, she thought she saw heat flare in those ice-blue eyes. But it faded as quickly as it came, and she convinced herself it was only her imagination. "An education," he said. "Talking points. A plan. I want to go back home with the framework of a proposal I can present to Parliament. A plan for amending our constitution, as well as a rationale to support the proposal."

She nodded slowly. "Why?"

"Considering you wrote that paper, I imagine you already know."

"My paper wasn't specific to Avelle-am-see."

Technically, that was true. But as he studied her face, she was certain he knew exactly what had prompted her to choose an international law topic for her Law Review article.

To his credit, he didn't call her out on it. Instead, he simply said, "In my country, the monarch stands as head of the executive branch. A king who resembles your president, but with a bit more power, though it is balanced by the role and rights of the parliament.

She nodded. She already knew all of that, of course. It was amazing how much learning your ex-boyfriend was really a playboy prince could lead a girl down dozens of rabbit trails of research.

"In theory, I don't have a problem with the monarchy. Our country is small, and the royal family is not only integral to our identity, but it also acts as the underpinnings of tourism, which is essential to our economy."

"But?"

"But I do have a problem with our particular system."

"Agnatic primogeniture. Only a male heir can inherit the crown."

He nodded. One quick tip of his head.

"You think you're incompetent." She raised a brow as she looked him up and down, then shrugged carelessly. "I could see that."

To his credit, he didn't take the bait. "My sister is the first born, and she's a natural leader. As far as I'm concerned, she's being denied her birthright."

"Others would say it's your birthright."

"And they would be correct under the law as it now stands. But it's not my ambition."

"Physics," she said, remembering his passion. The way his face had lit up when he talked about his work with Professor Malkin.

He said nothing, and she wondered at his silence, but didn't ask. Instead, she straightened her shoulders and nodded. "I honestly don't know how much help I can be, but I can help you understand the issues, the arguments, the pros and cons so that you can go back and advocate for the change."

"That would be most helpful."

"But I have a price."

His brows rose. "Over and above your firm's already hefty hourly rate?"

"Yes."

The corner of his mouth twitched, but all he said was, "I'm listening."

"I … I have to speak. At the symposium. My father thinks … well, he's wrong. I'll … mess up, and it … it won't reflect … well on the firm. And my dad … I'll end up … disappointing him."

Leo looked at her for so long that she feared he would say no. Then he slowly nodded. "I can't help you with how to speak—you already know what to do. The breathing. The pacing."

She started to argue, but he continued, cutting her off.

"But I can work with you. I can help you become more comfortable in front of a group, so that you don't rush and so that your nerves don't get the better of you. In this instance, I think that is key."

He wasn't wrong. "You'd do that?"

"In exchange for your help?" He met her eyes, his expression unreasonable. "Yes, Skye. I will do that."

He smiled, and her stomach flipped over. And right then, Skye wasn't sure if she'd gotten the help she needed, or if she'd set herself up for heartbreak all over again.

Chapter Twelve

"BE CAREFUL, SIRE."

Leopold turned to Jürgen. "Sire?"

His friend shrugged, then spoke in their native tongue. "In my official capacity, I feel I must remind you that anything more than helping Ms. Porter prepare for her speech could prove to be … difficult."

His friend wasn't wrong, but that didn't mean Leopold appreciated the reminder. More importantly, he knew that nothing would happen between him and Skye. Or, rather, nothing physical, despite the visceral longing he felt whenever he was near her.

That, however, would be a bad idea for so many reasons. Even so, he did hope that by working together he could make amends for hurting her. He could never completely make it up to her, but perhaps this time together would at least begin to heal the wounds he'd inflicted.

"I appreciate the concern, though I assure you it isn't necessary."

Jürgen looked about to argue, but held his tongue.

"You can go back to the hotel," Leopold said as he entered Skye's building, a tall glass box dotted with balconies overlooking the Austin skyline or the river. They'd agreed to meet at her condo at seven, though he had no intention of staying there. Being alone with her would only make things more difficult. Besides, if he wanted to help her, he needed someplace where they could find an audience.

"I'll escort you up, Sire."

"That's not necessary."

The elevator doors opened, and Leopold stepped on. So did Jürgen.

"The hotel. Now."

His security chief merely stared him down.

"Do you honestly believe someone is waiting outside Skye's condo to take me down? Even the press doesn't know I'm here."

"Yet," Jürgen said. "I imagine they will soon. Besides, you know that I don't have a choice, Sire. Not any more than you do."

Leopold scowled, but didn't argue. Jürgen might be the head of Leopold's security detail, but he answered to the king, not the prince. "At least be discreet."

"I shall endeavor to be invisible, Sire."

Leopold ignored his friend and pushed the button for Skye's floor. They rode in silence, with Jürgen stepping down the hall as Leopold headed for the door. "Aren't you afraid there's an assassin waiting to jump me in there?"

"Considering how Skye feels about you now, I wouldn't be surprised." He held up a hand as if in apology; Leopold knew that Jürgen and Skye had become friends two years ago. Hurting her hadn't sat well with him. "I will wait here."

"Thanks." Leopold took a breath, then rang the bell. He heard the footsteps approaching, then the door opened and Skye stood there, her face alight with laughter.

"Sorry. I was just—something funny. It doesn't matter."

But it did, because it suited her. He'd forgotten how beautiful she was when she laughed. Until now, he'd yet to see pure joy on her face during this trip.

She ushered him in, then closed the door behind him, leaving Jürgen alone in the hall. Not that Leopold cared. He was just glad they had this moment alone.

"—and that's when Larry said. *Oh.*"

The voice was as full of laughter as Skye's expression—and was decidedly male.

So maybe they weren't so alone after all.

"Um, sorry." The man had golden hair and the kind of pecs that would put Jürgen's to shame. Leopold knew that because the only thing the man was wearing was the navy blue towel wrapped around his hips.

"Sorry," he said, looking at Skye. "I didn't realize we had company."

We.

"This is Leo," Skye said. "He's here to help me with my talk for the symposium. I told you, remember? Leo," she continued, her attention turning to him, "this is Bart. My … boyfriend."

The word hit Leopold like a knife.

Across the room, Bart's eyes widened. "Boyfr—"

Bart cut himself off with a chuckle, then shook his head before hooking his arm around Skye. "She's supposed to be introducing me as *her fiancé* now. Right, honeybun?"

Her smile was tight but teasing. "Not until you buy me the ring, sweetie."

He laughed then moved to kiss her on the forehead, but she backed away, waving an unadorned left hand. "Ring first, then the kisses."

Bart pressed a hand over his heart, pulled an exaggerated frown, then looked at Leo. "You always hurt the ones you love."

"So I've heard." Leopold cleared his throat,

shooting a sideways glance toward Skye. "But, ah, we really should get going."

"Going?" Her brow furrowed. "Aren't we … practicing here?"

"What good would that do? You're already comfortable speaking to me. And presumably you have no qualms about speaking to your fiancé."

"He makes a good point, snugglemuffins," Bart said.

Skye's smile was almost a grimace. Leopold wasn't surprised. There was a time and place for pet names, and frankly he would prefer that time and place not be here and now. "Thanks for your input, honey."

"Shall we?" Leopold asked. He hoped she said yes. Otherwise he might have to text Jürgen to pull the fire alarm simply as an escape plan. But then the media might show up, and he might get photographed. Definitely not the best plan.

"Sure," she said, blowing a kiss too Bart. "Don't wait up and don't worry. I have an excellent chaperone."

Bart blew a kiss back, and Leopold was grateful to escape the treacle. Jürgen followed them onto the elevator, acknowledging Skye only with a nod. "I had no idea you were engaged," Leopold said as the elevator descended. He caught the rise of Jürgen's brows, but kept his attention on Skye.

"Why would you?"

A good question, and one he couldn't answer honestly. Over the years, he'd kept tabs on her career and, he'd thought, her personal life. He knew she had a male roommate, but he'd assumed that they were only friends. He'd never allowed his team to poke around too closely in her life. Now, he regretted maintaining that distance.

Except, no, he didn't. Or at least he shouldn't. There was no future between them. Even if it weren't impossible because of his inevitable coronation, the fact that he walked out on her would be enough to cool the most red-hot of romances.

The unfortunate and inescapable reality was that Skye could never be his. And in light of that fact, he knew that he should be happy for her to have found a man she loved. One she was so clearly comfortable with. Who teased her and laughed with her.

Yes, he was happy for her. Giddy, even. Absolutely, he was.

"—getting off?"

He frowned; those weren't exactly words he was expecting.

"Are we getting off?" Skye repeated, nodding toward the open elevator doors.

"Yes. Of course." He stepped to the side, allowing her to exit first, then followed. Jürgen flashed a knowing smirk, then fell in step behind them.

"Where … are we going?"

"Not far," Leopold said, still pulling himself together. "Come on."

He led her through downtown to his hotel, then across the lobby to the marble stairs that led up to the Driskill Bar, an atmospheric venue with dark wooden paneling, leather furniture, and bronze sculptures. A pianist was playing soft music, and he led her to a small table for two. Jürgen settled himself on one of the barstools. Far enough away to give them privacy. Close enough to keep an eye on Leopold should a random assassin decide to pop in and take a shot.

"I love this place," Skye said once they were settled. "It feels like something … out of another era. Like a speak … easy."

"You don't mind?"

"Mind what?"

"Being alone with me."

"Why would I?"

"You're engaged. Bart doesn't mind?"

She glanced down at the tabletop. "This is work. Isn't it?" When she lifted her head, he saw the question in her eyes.

"Of course." He was about to press further when the waiter arrived. "I'll let you order for both of us," he told Skye, who scowled, but didn't argue.

"Garrison Brothers," she told the woman. "One … ice cube for me. Neat for … him."

"Appetizers?"

"Fries … please."

"You got it." The woman turned, her blond ponytail swinging.

"You sounded fine," he said. "Clear and confident."

She shook her head. "She could have … driven to Dallas … in those pauses."

"That's her problem, not yours. You were the one ordering—that pays her bills. And in two weeks, you'll be the one delivering valuable information to me and everyone else at the symposium. That means you're the one with the power."

"Not according to … my dad."

"What? The client is always right? That may be true later in the relationship, but not when you're sharing knowledge. We need you, Skye. That gives you power."

She licked her lips, and that simple swipe of her tongue set off a chain reaction of memories that had him gripping the arms on his chair to forestall a very inappropriate groan. *This woman.* No one had ever affected him the way she had—and still did. And right then he hated the universe for the cruel game it had played with the two of them.

He cleared his throat. "So, I should apologize for my manners. I believe I owe you congratulations."

"You do? *Oh.* About Bart. Yes. Thank you."

"How long have you two been together?"

She cocked her head, her eyes narrowing as she studied him. "Why are you here, Leo?"

"I believe the term is extortion. You extracted a price for working with me, remember?"

She didn't laugh. "I mean at all. With all of our history, why come to me? So what if I wrote that paper? It was just a Law Review article. There is nothing in there that hundreds of attorneys across the globe couldn't counsel you on. What?" she added, when he didn't answer right away, just smiled.

"Your words were a bit muddled, but your pauses were significantly less. You regulated your breathing, and it worked."

The return of the waiter gave her a reprieve before answering. She swirled the glass, then took a sip. "I was talking to you."

"And I don't make you nervous?"

She seemed to genuinely consider the question. "No," she said. "You never have."

He started to reach for her hand, remembered, and pulled back. He cleared his throat. "I'm glad to hear it."

"You still haven't … answered my question. Why me when any lawyer would do?"

"That's not a question you should have to ask."

She looked down, then ran her finger over the rim of her glass. "Leo. Don't. Just … don't."

"I am sorry, Skye. More sorry than you'll ever know. Or believe."

"Why wouldn't I believe you? Just because you … walked away after the first time we finally slept together? Because you never … called? Because I … learned that not only were you a … prince, but you were … prancing around Europe with a dozen … girls on your arm."

This time her speech wasn't clear. The words came painfully slow, their tones slurring together so that he had to concentrate to understand her.

"I am sorry. At first, I was frantic. My father had a heart attack, and I was about to inherit the throne. I couldn't—I couldn't *be* with you. I knew that. And I was so angry at the world and my fate that I pushed that reality down, burying myself in the minutiae of duty."

"You're saying you didn't … call me because you … wanted me?"

The dysarthria did nothing to mask the sarcasm. He heard that loud and clear.

"I was an idiot. And then—I don't know. Once my father was well, I could have come back. I could have flown to Texas and told you everything."

"But you didn't."

"No."

"I see." She took another sip of whiskey. She'd barely made a dent.

He picked up his glass and downed the rest of his.

"So you're here now … with me … because you need to learn about amending your constitution."

He knew he ought to say yes. Whatever had been between them was gone—and if it wasn't, it might as well be. Even if he hadn't hurt her, they had no future.

But he didn't say yes. Instead, he told her the truth. "I'm here because Professor Malkin is getting an award on Friday. Your firm's symposium was a happy coincidence."

"So you could have just hired another attorney?"

"Could have, yes. Probably should have."

"But you didn't." She stirred her whiskey with her fingertip, then sucked the liquid off.

"No," he said, his entire body tightening. "I didn't."

She withdrew the digit, her cheeks pink.

"I was coming to Austin. You'd written this article. Your firm was hosting an international law symposium. The coincidence seemed too much to ignore."

"Quantum entanglement," she said, then grinned.

He realized he was smiling. "Not exactly, but I'm proud of you for trying."

"Well, I never was the physicist."

"No." He reached for her hand, and she didn't withdraw it. "You're right that I could have asked another lawyer. Maybe I should have. But I wanted you."

"Why?" Her voice was barely a whisper.

"Because you'd already helped me once, so I hoped you could help me again."

"I did? How?"

"You fell for me, and not my crown. And back then, that mattered more than you can know."

Chapter Thirteen

SKYE PACED the living room as Bart sat on the couch watching her, probably thinking she was crazy.

He caught her eye as she reached the wall, turned around, and started back toward the kitchen. "Did you tell him you're happily engaged, and that he needs to keep his distance?"

Skye paused, then shrugged. "I didn't tell him that I'm not."

"Good. He thinks we're together. That's a good plan. That's solid. It'll make everything go more smoothly while you two are working together."

Skye nodded, though with less enthusiasm than she probably should have. Somehow the idea that Leo believed she was unavailable just depressed her.

"You're meeting him again tomorrow night, right?"

"Bart?"

"What?"

"I don't want to be engaged."

"Hannah," Bart called toward the kitchen. "You want to help me out?"

"Like hell," Hannah called back. "You giving relationship advice? I'm all ears."

Bart scowled, then sighed. Then he scooted to the side of the couch, angling his body as he looked at Skye and patted the seat next to him. "We need to have a conversation."

With a sigh, she went and sat, curling her feet up beneath her.

"What happened to being wildly pissed off?"

"I was. Maybe I still am. I don't know." She'd been fiddling with her hands, but now she looked up at him. "He was so … earnest. So sorry."

"Earnest? Can royalty be earnest?"

She ignored him. "I think he genuinely felt horrible … about what happened. I want ... I really like him. Maybe I even love him. Or loved him before."

"Skye…"

"I don't like being angry at him. It feels … wrong."

"Okay. I get that. You're not someone who holds a grudge." Bart reached out and took her hand. "But that doesn't mean you should go all in with this guy. Come on, Skye. He's a prince.

Remember? It's not like this is going to go anywhere."

"That's not … a good reason for me to stay mad. I mean … why shouldn't I forgive him? Like you said, this can't go anywhere. He's a prince. And I'm … just me. But we have a … connection. And I don't want to destroy that by holding onto being angry."

"Damn right, he's a prince. Which means he's supposed to be held to a higher standard of how to treat people. You're totally justified in being angry."

"Oh please," Hannah said, walking back in from the kitchen holding three open bottles of beer. She handed them out as she asked, "What tabloids have you been reading? Higher standard? The rich and royals are users."

"No," Skye protested. "He's..."

"*But,*" Hannah said firmly, "Leo sounds like a good one. I mean if nothing else, he's trying to stay on the down low. He's not out there being a social media whore, right?"

Bart stared at Hannah, then turned to Skye. "What's going on here? Yesterday you were furious with him."

"I know. I was. Maybe I still am." She stood and started pacing again, her emotions all in a muddle. "I had a good time tonight. And he—"

"He hurt you. Like deeply."

"He apologized." She looked between her

friends. "And it was a real apology. Shouldn't that count for something?"

"Of course," Hannah said.

"Why are you not helping me on this?" Bart demanded.

Hannah shrugged, and Bart leaned his head back and groaned.

Skye dropped back onto the couch again, then faced him. "So you're saying … I should still be angry with … you because of that time you washed all my … sweaters on hot?"

"I didn't realize—"

"Or that time you took me to that kara … oke bar and you were so … drunk that you insisted I sing? And the crowd …started jeering me?" She shuddered. That had been one of the more mortifying moments in her life.

"Yeah, but I was really drunk, and—"

"You're one of my best … friends, Bart. I forgave you. Of course I forgave you."

Bart leaned back with a sigh. "But he's not one of your best friends, is he? He's a man you could fall in love with. And that's going to make everything different."

Skye swallowed, wanting to argue, but there wasn't anything to say.

She met Hannah's eyes, and saw the resignation there, too.

They all three knew the bottom line—Leo could hurt her again.

The only question now was if she was willing to take the risk.

Skye spent Saturday afternoon burning off energy by cleaning the apartment while listening to an audio-book on the history of Avelle-am-see. She lasted three hours before she couldn't stand it anymore and switched over to an Eighties mix on Spotify.

She was jamming to *You Shook Me All Night Long* with a rag and a spray bottle of Clorox cleaner, when she twirled out of the bathroom and ran straight into Leo. She gasped, yanking the head-phones out of her ears. "How did you get in here?"

"Your fiancé let me in."

It took her a second to process the fiancé part. "Oh. Right. What time is it? I'm so sorry I'm not even ready. I was just cleaning. I must've lost track of time."

"Don't worry. It's only four."

"I thought we were going out at seven."

"We are. I was supposed to go over to Professor Malkin's house for a quick drink this afternoon, but his little girl is sick. I thought I would take a chance and come by here since my afternoon opened up."

"Oh. I'm so sorry." Except she wasn't. She wasn't sorry at all.

"It's probably just a cold, but he didn't want to risk me catching it. Honestly, neither did I." His mouth twisted and he managed a small shudder.

"What?"

"Trust me when I say that being a royal with a cold is a miserable experience."

"Over-tending?"

"The entire palace staff walks on eggshells and tries to make me feel better. It's exhausting."

She laughed, enjoying the moment until he turned that sexy smile toward her. Then the happiness shifted, and a wave of shyness crashed over her. She put the rag and cleaner on the coffee table, then had nothing to do with her hands. She shoved them in the pocket of her ratty shorts, then realized that she was only wearing flannel sleep shorts and a threadbare white tank top that was practically see-through.

"Um, well, it's good to see you." She thought about crossing her arms over her chest, but decided that would make the predicament more obvious.

"I thought we could get a little bit more work in."

"Sure. Just let me get dressed. We can head on over … to my office and start planning how you can advocate for amending the … constitution. I was listening to the history of Avelle-am-see while I was cleaning, and I think—"

"I didn't realize that our history was quite so bouncy. You managed quite an interesting number with your hips."

She cleared her throat, certain her cheeks were burning. "You saw that?"

He just grinned.

"I, um, switched over to a rock playlist."

"Don't tell me you got bored listening to my country's history. I'm shocked."

She laughed outright. "In my defense, before I switched over to AC/DC, I learned a lot. Your country … prided itself on equal rights for women early on. The constitution is … an anomaly, and I think the citizens will … support you. We just need to—"

"All that's fascinating. But you need to tell me later."

"Later?"

"Right now we're going to the zoo. Then The Fix."

"The zoo?"

She expected him to tell her that he was joking. But soon enough they were in his rented Porsche and heading toward the Austin Zoo, a non-profit rescue zoo for a variety of species. It was one of Skye's favorite places, but it didn't meet some people's expectations. "You know that Austin's zoo is … small, right? If you're looking to … visit a traditional zoo, we need to go all the way to San … Antonio or up to Waco."

"Trust me," Leo said. "Smaller is better for our purposes."

"Our purposes?"

But he didn't answer. He just cranked up the radio to an '80s rock station, then grinned at her. "I thought we'd keep with your theme for the day."

She laughed, and they jammed the rest of the way there, singing along with Def Leppard, Van Halen, and Queen. She lost herself in the music and the laughter, and didn't even worry about how she sounded or what he had in mind.

It wasn't until they were on the premises that he explained his plan, which was how she ended up standing in front of the genet habitat while the adorable, cat-like creatures relaxed on the tree-branches and makeshift hammocks. Slowly and deliberately, she read the information plaque to a blond-haired six-year-old who listened intently before telling his mother he wanted to take one home.

After the genets, they moved on to bobcats—good swimmers with "bobbed" tails, and thus the name—which she introduced to a nine-year-old who kept asking questions that she couldn't answer.

The three-year-old by the coatimundi habitat wasn't at all interested in the animals, but she read him the information card nevertheless. And on and on they went through the zoo, with Skye reading the various information plaques to the children who gathered nearby.

By the time she'd spoken to the fifth or sixth kid, she'd stopped being self-conscious. It was clear that the kids didn't notice her slurred and hesitant speech. As for the parents, if they noticed, they didn't mention it, probably relieved to have some of the educational tasks taken off their shoulders.

"Thanks," she said to Leo as they walked back to his car. "That was fun."

"I'm glad you thought so. Best of all, you've earned a drink."

They headed back downtown, followed by Jürgen who'd been discreetly tailing them all day. "Doesn't he mind?" Skye asked, turning around to watch as Jürgen's Range Rover crossed two lanes to slide in behind Leo's Porsche.

"Mind? No. It's his job. He's a friend, yes, but he's responsible for my safety. Normally, he'd be in the car with me. Today though...."

"I guess I … should be flattered. He obviously doesn't … think that I'm out to kill you."

Leo shot her a quick grin. "When we first came back to the States, that remained an open question."

"Rightfully so," she said with a teasing grin. "But not anymore?"

"No," she said, meeting his eyes. "Not anymore." They shared a smile before the light changed, and he inched forward in the downtown traffic. "I'm very glad to hear it."

She stayed silent as he left the car with the valet at the Driskill. They walked the short distance from the hotel to The Fix, with Jürgen pacing them from about half a block behind.

"You know," she said, trying to sound casual, "that really was fun. You should take Talia to the zoo. Just don't make her read the plaques, and it could be a fabulous date."

He paused on the sidewalk in front of The Fix, turning to face her directly. "Have you ever gone there with Bart?"

She shook her head. He nodded, then held the door open for her. They walked in silence until they were settled at a two top near the stage where a local band was playing country music. Fortunately, they weren't too loud, and it was easy to talk. "I owe you an apology," Leo said as soon as he'd ordered Loaded Coronas for both of them.

"You do? What for?"

His shoulders rose and fell as he sighed. Then he laid his hand on top of hers. "For letting you have the wrong impression. Talia's part of my publicity team."

"Oh." She pulled her hand away, suddenly all too aware of the brush of skin against skin. She put her hands in her lap and twisted her fingers together. "Well, you should be careful." She looked everywhere but directly at him. "Sleeping with someone on your team is the kind of thing that will draw bad press."

He nodded slowly. "True, but I should have been more clear. I'm not sleeping with her. She was wearing my shirt because she spilled coffee all over her blouse. I lent it to her so that we could have it washed while she went back to her apartment. She's not staying at the Driskill. She actually has family in town."

"Oh. Then why did you—?"

"I let you think that we were together because..."

She frowned as he trailed off. "Because why?"

He drew a noisy breath. "Because I knew it would add distance between us."

"Oh." She stiffened. "You want distance."

"No." He leaned forward. "No, I really don't. But I also didn't want to hurt you again, and that was before I knew you were engaged."

"Right. Of course." She cleared her throat. "Well, that's really sweet of you to protect me." She kept her hands tightly into her lap, realizing after a minute, that she was squeezing them so tightly that she was at risk of cutting off circulation to her fingers.

"Later, it didn't seem important to tell you.

After all, you're with Bart, so what did it matter? He seems like a nice guy, by the way. I'm happy for you."

"Yeah. He's one of the good ones." She flashed a bright smile, as if she was in the best relationship ever. But she couldn't sustain it.

"Skye?"

She sighed. "Look, he is nice. He's a great guy. But he's not mine."

"I'm sorry?"

"I guess we think alike," she said. "He's a friend from law school. And he's my roommate while his place is being remodeled. But there's nothing between us. There never has been."

"Well." Leo sat back, his head slightly cocked. "Isn't that interesting information?"

"Is it?"

He met her eyes, and she saw the depths of heat and longing there.

"Yes, Skye. I think it is."

Chapter Fourteen

"A DAIQUIRI?" Skye asked an hour later when she returned from the ladies' room. "What about another loaded Corona?"

Leo shook his head. "We've moved from drinking for pleasure to drinking as part of your instruction. Not that watching you suck on a straw won't be pleasurable for me..."

Skye rolled her eyes. "You want me to do oral motor exercises?"

"I can think of a lot of things I'd like you to do that are oral."

Skye had just drawn a sip of daiquiri through the straw, immediately started to laugh, then almost ended up choking. She put her hand up to stop Leo from coming to her side of the table, then shot him a narrow-eyed glance. "Are you flirting, Your Highness?"

"I might be. Now that we've cleared the air about girlfriends and fiancés." He grimaced. "I'm sorry. I shouldn't flirt."

She bit her lower lip, knowing she should stay silent. But instead she said, "It's okay. I kind of like it."

"Kind of?"

"I like it," she said definitively. "And I know—I know it's not going … anywhere. I … see the whole big picture. I may not sound like it, but I'm … actually pretty smart."

"Don't do that." His voice had gone hard, and she didn't have to ask what he meant. But he was wrong. She'd been judged her entire life on how she sounded to people. Most of the time she minded, but in her more lucid moments, she told herself that it gave her an advantage. After all, opposing counsel usually didn't see her coming.

Not that she had that many judgey encounters in the first place. For the most part, she'd locked herself in an ivory tower, one her father was now trying to drag her from.

For the first time in a long time, she felt a niggle of regret for the choices she'd made. Because every once in a while, she did want to be out there, talking and educating. And while she knew that the kids at the zoo weren't a good representation of what other attorneys and clients could be like, the experience had been a positive one.

Both the parents and the kids had appreciated what she'd done, and seeing the fascination on the children's faces as she told them the fun facts reflected on the various plaques around the zoo had been worth whatever discomfort she'd felt talking aloud.

She looked at Leo, only to find him studying her as well. Their eyes met and held, and she felt a familiar shiver cut through her. He'd always affected her that way, from the first moment she'd seen him in this very bar two years ago. It was like they were the quantum particles he studied, with an undeniable attraction between them.

Without breaking his gaze, she wrapped her lips around the straw and drew in a long sip of the daiquiri. The muscle in his jaw tightened, and he pressed his lips together, his knuckles turning white as he clutched the edge of the table.

She sucked harder, feeling flirty and powerful, then pulled her mouth away and slowly licked her lips.

"You're trying to kill me."

She laughed. "Should I take another sip?"

He shook his head. "You better not. I don't want Jürgen to have to take you down for attempted regicide."

She waved the words away. "Oh, please. You're not the king yet."

"Thank God for that." He shook his head.

"Even so, best we don't get too worked up." He met her eyes. "Yet."

"Yet?" Her skin prickled with both anticipation and trepidation. "What do you mean?"

"We came here for a reason, Skye. And more than just sipping frozen drinks through a straw."

"Oh." She wrinkled her nose.

"Don't worry. You'll survive. And I promise I reward good effort."

Those butterflies were back in her stomach, but she nodded. "I'm up for … anything."

He flashed a panty-dropping grin. "I'm very glad to hear that." Then he lifted his hand, and Tyree, the bar's founder, came striding toward them holding a clipboard. "You're about to go announce the drink and appetizer specials," Leo told her.

"Well, that just killed the mood." She scowled at him, but he only laughed.

"You're welcome."

She rolled her eyes, then laughed, but couldn't deny that she actually was a little bit sad. The mood had been going exactly where she wanted it to … even though she knew that she shouldn't want it to go that direction at all.

Tyree had paused at the table next to theirs, but came over now. He wore jeans and a white T-shirt that both contrasted his dark skin and highlighted the military and other tattoos that covered his arms. "You ready, sugar?" he asked, his Cajun accent thick. With his broad shoulders and well-muscled body, he looked like he could be the bar's bouncer, and a damn good one at that, but he was one of the most gentle men she'd ever meet.

"You sure you want me to do this? This is going to reflect on your place."

Tyree only laughed and shook his head. "Nice try, sugar. This bar has been through a lot. I don't think you're going to be the one who makes it crash and burn around our ears."

"I wouldn't be so sure," she said, and although she was perfectly serious, Tyree and Leo just chuckled.

She looked around the customers who would be her audience, searching out familiar faces. Unfortunately, most of her friends weren't there tonight. Griffin and his fiancé, Beverly, had been in earlier, but they seemed to have disappeared. And Jenna and Reese, both co-owners of The Fix, were nowhere to be seen. Hannah wasn't there either, which meant that the only moral support she had lay with these two men.

Skye grimaced. At least she'd only be making a fool of herself in front of strangers. She took the clipboard from Tyree, drew a deep breath, and climbed up onto the stage. The mic was already set up on a stand, and when she got there, she smiled nervously. Usually, one of the waiters did this on a daily basis, so she knew the drill. She just never expected that she'd be the one doing the announcing.

She cleared her throat, then leaned toward the microphone. "Um ... hi. It's ... time for you to hear ... the specials." She looked for and found Leo's eyes. He was looking back at her, nodding encouragement, but she knew that she sounded like a train wreck.

Her nerves were getting the better of her, and she was having a hell of a time regulating her breathing. She wanted to hate him for doing this to her, but she also knew that she needed it. There was no way she was going to survive presenting at the symposium if she couldn't even talk about a drink and an appetizer in a bar where nobody was listening that closely and half the folks were buzzed. Some were probably even so drunk that they sounded more slurry than she did.

So, yeah. She could do this thing. And she wanted to, if only to make Leo proud.

Once again, she cleared her throat, then concentrated on breathing and slowing her speech. "Right. So, today's drink … special is the Jalapeño … Margarita. And if … you want a truly … hot time … try … pairing it with … our Pimento Cheese … Poppers. You'll love … the kick."

She was starting to sweat, and she knew that the words had become so slurred that anyone interested was having to concentrate to understand. She met

Leo's eyes, feeling trapped, but he only smiled and nodded encouragement.

Right. She was almost done. She could finish this. Even if she'd have to throw her blouse away after since no way were the sweat stains coming out. "Both are … fifty … percent off. So enjoy."

"Great pitch, cutie," someone called from the back. "You already drunk on the things?"

Tears pricked her eyes, and she hurried off the stage, only then realizing that Leo wasn't at their table anymore. Instead, he had his hand wrapped around the heckler's collar and had hauled him up out of his chair.

"I've got this," Tyree said, putting a calming hand on Leo's shoulder. "That's no way to talk to a lady," he said to the drunken creep, his voice soft but firm. "I think it's time for you to leave."

The man protested, but Skye didn't catch all of his words. She was already hurrying to the restroom at the back of the bar. And about the time she heard the applause—presumably for Tyree kicking the guy out—she closed the door and locked herself inside.

There was a sharp knock on the door a moment later. "Hey," Leo said. "It's me. Can you let me in?"

She almost didn't, but right then what she craved more than anything was to be in his arms. She pushed away from the sink where she'd been bent over, willing the tears to stop, then unlocked the door. The moment he opened it, she fell into his embrace.

"I'm sorry," she said when she'd stopped crying. "I got … your shirt all wet."

"No. I'm the one who's sorry. I shouldn't have put you up to that. I didn't think there would be anyone in the audience who was that much of a prick."

"It's not your … fault. I shouldn't care so much. And you're … right. He's the one who's the … asshole."

"Of course you should care. I care, too."

It was such an honest and unexpected response. Most people tried to tell her that she shouldn't care. That she should learn to just blow it off and push through it. They didn't understand that would never happen. She would always care. It would always hurt. The trick was learning how to handle the hurt.

Leo got that. Maybe it was because he lived his life in public, but somehow he truly understood. And before she could think about what she was doing, she lifted herself up on her toes, hooked her arms around his neck, and kissed him.

Chapter Fifteen

OH, dear God, how he'd missed this.

The power of her kiss exploded through him, firing his senses, making him crave what he knew he shouldn't take.

"Please."

Skye's whisper filled his head, the need in her voice acting like a drug, stealing thought and reason.

"Skye—"

She drew back, then pressed a finger to his lips. Her eyes were puffy from crying, but they no longer looked wounded. Now, they were filled with a passion and need so palpable that it made his skin tingle.

"Please," she whispered. "Take me back to your room."

He swallowed, his mouth going dry. He was as

hard as steel, and all he could think about was touching her, *taking* her. But they shouldn't, not when there was no future for them.

"We can't," he said. "You know we can't."

She slid her hand down, cupping his cock and making him groan from the force of the pure, feral need that cut through him. "Can't? I don't think so."

"Shouldn't." He could barely croak out the word.

"Why not?" She bit her lower lip, her expression a delightful mix of shyness and certainty. "We both want it."

"And we both know it will end. That it will have to end."

"Isn't that all the more … reason to take what we can? If I … can't have you … I at least want … this."

He stroked her hair, his eyes not leaving hers. "You're amazing."

"We deserve … the memory."

His grin was ironic. "I supposed we do. A better one than last time."

There was no pain or judgment when she shook her head, but a single tear snaked down her cheek. "Last time … was amazing."

"I was your first." He heard the harshness in his voice, the recrimination. "And I left."

"You were my only … and it was wonderful."

It took a moment, but once the meaning of her words hit him, he stiffened. "Only?"

Her shoulders rose and fell in a casual shrug. "Who could compare to you?"

"Skye. I—"

Once again, she shushed him with her fingertip. "No … I wasn't … pining. I was studying and working. And dating … is hard, what with … this," she said, pointing to her mouth. "But … I know it … was different … for you. I … became a … royal watcher."

"Oh, God."

"Quite the player."

Her tone was teasing, but he rushed to explain. She deserved the truth. Hell, she was the only one who did.

"I never slept with any of them."

Her brow furrowed, and then she laughed.

"I'm serious." Eventually, he probably would have taken one of them to bed, but how could he when Skye was so fresh in his mind and still alive in his heart? Two years wasn't that long in the grand scheme of things, and he'd been mourning the inevitable certainty that one day he would sit on the throne alone, because even if he did find a woman to be his queen, it wouldn't be the woman he craved.

She was staring at him as if he'd gone crazy. "But I read—"

"I drank and I partied. I acted like an ass. My father survived, for which I was terribly grateful, but his heart attack was a wake-up call."

"That's why you left that night. You never told me. Never called or anything."

"I was angry at the world, furious about the golden chains that shackled me, and I took it out on you. I'm sorry. I can't ever make it right, but I am truly sorry."

She brushed a light kiss over his lips. "I forgive you. And," she added with a mischievous grin, "if you take me back to your hotel you can at least try to make it better."

He burst out laughing. "God, I love you."

The reality of his words hit them both at the same time. Her eyes were wide, her lips parted. He could see the way her T-shirt moved with the pounding of her heart.

"It's true," he whispered. "I wish it wasn't, because one day I will be king, and my choices for who can be my queen are limited. And even if it could be you..." He trailed off, blinking back the tears that had gathered in his eyes, "how could I ask you to live such a public life?"

She swallowed, her lips parting as if to speak, but no words came.

"And so I rebelled. I partied. I acted like an ass. But I never slept with any of them. They never got into my heart. There's only ever been you, Skye."

Tears streaked her face now, and she shook her head. "There can't just … be me. Leo, you're … breaking my heart. I don't … want that for … you."

"Being royal has its perks, I won't deny that. But fate balances the scales. I accepted that a long time ago."

She moved closer, her arms going around his waist, her body pressed against his. "That's why we … deserve tonight. These … weeks. To fit in a … lifetime before you … have to leave."

"Skye, we—"

But she didn't let him finish. Just silenced him with a kiss before pulling back and meeting his eyes. She held his gaze, hers unreadable. Then she slid down his body, her fingers making quick work of the button on his jeans.

"Christ, Skye, what are you doing?"

"Isn't it obvious?" She was on her knees, her head tilted back, her eyes dancing with mischief. "You had me sucking a straw earlier … and you said being … royal sucks. Might as well add a little … more truth to that statement."

He would have protested, but when she took him in her mouth, he knew that he was both the luckiest and the unluckiest man in the entire world.

Because how was he supposed to go back home without her?

Chapter Sixteen

SKYE PRACTICALLY DANCED out of the ladies' room on Leo's arm. She felt giddy. Powerful. And Leo seemed pretty happy himself.

"You're looking quite smug," Leo said, his voice teasing.

"I feel … smug. I've never done that before."

Leo's brows rose. "I believe you have."

She bit back a laugh, remembering their night together two years ago.

"Fine. Never in a bathroom at a bar, I mean."

"Well, that's two of us."

She glanced around as they walked hand in hand back to their table, noticing the girls sitting nearby, watching and giggling.

"Do you think they know what we were doing?" Skye whispered the question, feeling partly embarrassed and at the same time weirdly proud and powerful.

"Possibly," Leo admitted. "But they might also be watching because I almost punched that guy. A bar fight tends to draw attention."

Her stomach twisted as she realized the implications. "Leo—you…" She trailed off. He'd put himself out there for her, and that had been a mistake. Those girls probably *were* taking his picture, and if they were posting about the hot guy doing macho stuff in a bar, then the odds were good that someone would recognize him.

She drew a breath, saying a silent prayer despite knowing it would do no good whatsoever.

At the door, Jürgen fell in step beside them. Skye glanced at him and knew that her fears weren't stupid. His brow was furrowed, and he was frowning at his phone. And considering his sole purpose was to keep Leo safe, she had a feeling she knew what he was frowning about.

"We should go back to the hotel, Sire."

"We are," Leo said, squeezing Skye's hand. If he was thinking about the possible public relations nightmare or the blowing of his cover in Austin, he wasn't showing it.

They walked to the corner in silence, Jürgen settling in several paces behind them.

"Maybe you should just walk me home," she whispered, because he needed a way out. *Surely* he realized the risk. She didn't want him to feel obligated to continue their evening when it could blow up his whole life. If they hadn't already blown it up.

God, what had she started?

"Back to your condo?"

She nodded. "It's late." It wasn't even ten. She sounded like an idiot.

"I could walk you home," he said easily. "You could spend the rest of the evening watching TV with Bart." He squeezed her hand, then tugged her to a stop as he leaned closer to whisper in her ear. "Or I could invite you to my room, strip you bare, and make love to you. Personally, I'm leaning toward the latter."

"Leo—those girls."

"Aren't welcome in my room."

She couldn't hold back the laughter that bubbled up. "Glad to … hear that."

"Are you with me?"

She nodded, her throat thick. "Always."

They'd reached the hotel, and he led her inside, then to the small elevator bank. They rode up with Jürgen, fingers twined, and as soon as the car stopped, she took a step forward, eager to be alone with him in the room.

But then the doors slid open, and she was blinking as those same girls from the bar giggled and snapped photos. She had no idea how they'd discovered what floor he was on—they'd probably just guessed the penthouse—and they were breathless from what was undoubtedly a race up the stairs.

She froze, Leo's hand tightening on hers as he stepped protectively in front of her.

Skye had no idea how he managed to get out so quickly, but Jürgen was not only already in the hallway, but he'd wrested the phones away from both the girls.

"Hey! You can't do that!"

"This floor is for guests only." He tapped on both screens, scowled, tapped some more, then handed the phones back. "Go," he said. "Go now."

One girl looked ready to protest, but the other took her arm and they raced toward the stairs.

"I deleted all photos from the bar until now," Jürgen said. "But they'd already posted several. I can't do anything about what's already out there. This isn't good, Sire."

"I've been labeled as a bad boy prince at home for years. I'm just expanding my territory."

"It's not good for Skye," Jürgen said.

Beside her, Leo sighed. "No. It's not." He dragged his fingers through his hair, looking defeated. As far as Skye was concerned, the look didn't suit him at all.

"You should go," he said. "Jürgen can walk you to your condo."

"Leo, no."

He shook his head, his expression miserable. "I

can't drag you into the spotlight on this. That would be like forcing you to live your worst nightmare."

She shook her head. "No, you're wrong. You're my sweetest dream, Leo. That erases all the nightmares."

He took her hand and gently kissed her fingertips. "I am so glad that we found each other again, but we both know it can't last. It ends now, because I can't stand the thought that you'll be sacrificed on the altar of social media. I'm sorry, sweetheart. But you know I'm right."

He turned to Jürgen. "Get her home safely."

And then, his face colored with misery, the man she loved turned his back on her and disappeared into his suite.

Chapter Seventeen

"COME ON," Jürgen said, cocking his head toward the elevator.

Skye crossed her arms across her chest. "I don't think so."

"Skye. You heard His Highness. I'm to see you home."

"You can't … make me leave."

His brows rose. The man was seriously good-looking, but also imposing as hell. Skye congratulated herself on not caving.

"I'm staying."

"Don't make me use force."

"You wouldn't dare."

He took a step toward her, and she realized that, yeah, he'd totally dare. Whatever the prince wanted, Jürgen would do.

She sucked in a breath and decided to change her approach. "You … love him, too. Do you really want him to … be miserable?"

He crossed his arms over his massive chest and stared her down, as if he was just waiting for her to finish so he could toss her over his shoulder and carry her down to the street.

"You know he wants me there. And … we deserve it. He can't just … unilaterally stop it."

"He's my prince who will soon be my king. I think he can unilaterally do pretty much anything he wants."

"Including being an ass?"

Jürgen didn't smile, but his eyes flickered with amusement. Skye considered that a win.

"This thing can't … go anywhere. We're not … stupid. But I'm helping him with the constitution. And he's helping me … with my speech. So we're going … to be together anyway."

Jürgen said nothing. Another victory, as far as she was concerned.

"Tell me this—does he really love me? You're … one of his closest friends. If you tell me he doesn't, then I'll go away. But if he loves me, then don't we deserve to have whatever time we can grab?"

For a moment, Jürgen said nothing, just looked at her with those hooded eyes, his expression unreadable. Then he cleared his throat. He took a step toward her, and Skye held her breath, but managed to hold her ground.

"Do you love him?"

Skye drew in a breath, then managed a watery smile. "Is that really a question you have to ask?"

She watched as the decision played out over Jürgen's face. Then he reached into his jacket pocket and pulled out a key card. "If I get fired, I expect a job working security at your firm."

"You got it," she said, her knees weak with relief.

"And Skye…"

She was already at the door. Now, she looked back over her shoulder.

"You're good for him."

"He's good for me. Wish me luck?"

He tilted his head, and she turned back toward the penthouse. She drew a breath, inserted the card, then quietly stepped inside. There was no sign of Leo in the living area. She paused, her head tilting as she picked up the muffled sound of running water.

The shower.

Right. Well, that was a forward approach, wasn't it? Then again, he wouldn't kick her out if she was naked. Would he?

She stripped off her clothes, tossing them on the

ground on the far side of the sofa, just to make it more difficult for him to get rid of her.

Then she took a deep breath, stepped through the open door into the bedroom, and walked the short distance to the bathroom. The door was closed, but not locked. Why would it be? He was alone, after all.

She gently pushed the door open and was immediately lost in the thick, hot steam. She stood for a moment to get her bearings, then saw the glass shower stall. His back was to her, his face in the spray. She squared her shoulders, walked to the stall, and slowly pulled open the door.

She stepped in behind him, her hands settling on his hips. "Leo," she whispered even as he stiffened, one quick jolt of fear eclipsed by relief. And, she hoped, by longing.

She moved closer until her breasts were pressed against his back, and she slid her hands around to stroke his cock. His body tensed, and though she wanted to take him all the way, she wasn't disappointed when he spun around, one hand cupping her head as his mouth closed violently over hers. He pushed her back, his lips hard on hers, his tongue warring with her own. She felt the cool glass against her back in contrast to the wet heat of the shower—and to Leo's body, hot and hard and slick against hers.

"How are you here?"

His words were muffled by the press of his lips against her neck, then down lower until his teeth grazed her nipple. She made a squeaking noise, but couldn't manage a response.

"You shouldn't be here," he said, his hands belying his words as his palms stroked and teased, his fingers slipping between her thighs, the intimate touch making her body shake as she moaned.

"Do you mind?" She could barely force the words out past her gasps and the wild jolts of electricity that were firing through her body.

"Terribly," he said, as his hands slid to her hips and he lowered himself to his knees as he kissed his way down her belly. The tip of his tongue teased her clit, and her knees turned to rubber. She would have fallen except that he was holding her up, his entire mouth on her now, sucking and licking, and it felt so beyond incredible that it was a wonder she didn't pass out.

She twined her fingers in his hair and bucked against him, her body desperate for release even while her mind wanted this wild and delicious sensation to never, ever end.

"Please," she murmured, her mind so lost in a sensual haze that she wasn't even sure what she was asking for. He rose, and she whimpered, then melted again when he silenced her with a kiss.

"With me," he murmured, then led her out of

the shower, through the steamy bathroom, and to the pristinely made bed.

"We're soaking … wet."

"I don't care," he said, then pulled him down with her. He straddled her, his body so warm it was like he burned from within, erasing any fears that she'd be cold. On the contrary, she felt on fire, every cell in her body like a small generator, making her burn for him.

"Please," she begged. "Please, Leo, I don't want to wait."

He fumbled beside the bed, then pulled out a condom.

"I thought you said you … didn't." She meant it to be a tease, but maybe she was a tiny bit hurt that he'd told her he wasn't sleeping around, and yet he kept condoms in his drawer.

"I haven't," he said. He pushed himself up, then gently brushed her hair from her eyes. "But when I saw you again—I knew we shouldn't. I thought you wouldn't want me, anyway. And yet, I hoped."

She felt the tears prick her eyes. "Yes," she said. "I …hoped, too."

"Skye."

That was all he said, and their eyes locked and held. "Leo." His name was a whisper, but it held so much meaning. And so much hope.

His mouth closed over hers again, and she arched back as he claimed her with his kisses, his hand stroking her body, readying her until she was begging him, whimpering for him to please, please take her right then.

"As you wish," he whispered, then sank deep inside her as she arched up, meeting him thrust for thrust until they both exploded in a sizzle of stars and lightning and atoms and ecstasy. Until the world fell away, and it was just the two of them left, alone in each other's arms.

She clung to him, breathing hard and never wanting to let go.

"You're amazing," he whispered.

"I was just thinking the same thing," she said. "That, and that you'll probably have to call the front desk for a new duvet. This one got soaked."

He laughed, pulling her over until she was straddling him. "I'm sure they'll accommodate. I'm a prince, after all. Or hadn't you heard?"

"I think you mentioned something along those lines. And, Your Highness, I have to say that was incredible."

He brushed his fingertip over her lips. "Thank you," he said, the teasing gone from his voice. "For not listening to me. And for doing whatever you did that convinced Jürgen to let you in."

"Ah, yeah. Well, I … had to kill him. Sorry about that."

He stifled a laugh. "Well worth the sacrifice."

"Actually, I … owe him."

"We both do." He moved closer and kissed her again, and she never wanted the moment to end.

"It might get bad," he said, shattering the illusion.

"Or… it might not."

But, of course, it did.

Chapter Eighteen

"THIS IS UNACCEPTABLE," Tarlton Porter said, pacing behind his desk. "What the hell were you thinking? You, prancing around like some air-headed female?"

Skye forced herself not to cower as she looked at her father. "I'm not … air-headed, and I don't … prance. I love him."

Her father waved the words away as if they were gnats at a picnic. "I thought you knew better, Skye. This kind of behavior? And one week before the symposium? Did you even stop to think how this would reflect on the firm?"

"This is … my fault? I didn't ask to be … photographed. Followed. You're punishing me for … living my life."

For the last four days, she and Leo had been inseparable. They'd worked on the constitutional issues at the firm's library or the sitting area in his suite. They'd practiced her speaking with an audience from both the firm and Jürgen's security staff. They'd gone out for meals at both divey restaurants and high-end steak houses, with Skye always ordering to get in more practice. They'd had drinks at The Fix and mingled with her friends, all of whom accepted Leo as just one of the gang.

They hadn't gone out of their way to draw attention, but they hadn't tried to hide, either. True, they'd toned down the PDA, but there'd been handholding and a few kisses when they weren't behind closed door. They hadn't seen anyone taking snaps, but that didn't mean folks weren't watching. And considering the number of posts that had hit Twitter and other platforms, most royal watchers were very skilled at being sneaky. All the more impressive since Jürgen had stepped up security once the spotlight had landed on them.

"The man is a prince," her father said, both stating the obvious and drawing Skye from her thoughts. "He's used to a life of privilege. Of getting who he wants and what he wants."

"Is he? Well, so are you." She snapped the words out, fury making her react before thinking. But apparently her words hit the mark, because her father took a step backward.

"You're lashing out, Skye."

"You want … me to be someone … I'm not. And so you … insist I speak … at the symposium."

His shoulders sagged, and he settled into the chair behind his desk. She stood a bit longer, then took a seat, too. "I love him, Daddy. And he … loves me."

Her father sighed. "Let's say that's true."

"It is."

He didn't even pause for her comment. "It doesn't matter because nothing can come of it. The man is going to be a king. And soon if the reports about his father's health are accurate." He leaned forward. "Sweetheart, no matter how you feel about this man, you should end it."

She said nothing. He was right, of course. But she wasn't going to admit that aloud.

"What are you prepared to do if he wants you to go back with him? You're not royal. You're not a citizen. You can't marry him."

"You researched that?"

"You're my daughter. Of course, I did."

She blinked, fighting tears. "We know, Daddy."

"Tell me you aren't contemplating being his mistress."

She swallowed. The temptation was there, yes, if for no other reason than to stay with Leo. But she shook her head. "I couldn't be that girl." She managed a rueful smile, then shrugged. "But it doesn't matter anyway. I'd be in his circle no matter what, and I'd wither in the spotlight."

Her father stood then circled his desk. He stopped in front of her and held out his hand. She took it and rose, confused as to his purpose. "I'm so sorry," he said. "I tossed you into the symposium line-up thinking only of myself."

She swallowed, her throat suddenly thick with tears. "I don't know what you want from me, Daddy."

His shoulders sagged. "Oh, baby. All I want is your forgiveness."

A single tear escaped. "Then we've been at … cross purposes. Because all I've wanted is for you to … forgive yourself."

"One more week," Leo said as she snuggled close. They were in her bed, having gotten distracted when Skye was changing for the evening's celebration honoring Professor Malkin and his impressive body of work. "I have to leave right after the symposium. The royal physician has asked that Gisele and I both meet with him in person."

"I know. I don't want … you to go."

He looked at her, and she shook her head, certain she knew what he was going to say. She pressed her finger to his lips, then bent forward and kissed him. "We're going to enjoy the week … we have left."

"Yes," he said. "We are."

Her phone chimed, and she rolled over to find a text from Hannah about a possible client referral. As Skye started to type an answer, Leo slid out of bed, motioning that he was going to the kitchen.

She sent the reply and started to follow, only to stop when she heard the voices just beyond the door.

"Sleeping with my fiancée?" The humor in Bart's voice was clear.

"Hey, if you couldn't keep her satisfied…"

Skye clapped her hand over her mouth so as not to laugh aloud at Leo's response.

"A fair point," Bart said. "But, listen, I've got to say this, because I love her, too, you know? Not the way you do, but…"

"I get it."

"Yeah, well, for the record, you hurt her, and we're going to have issues."

"That's why I like you, man."

From behind the door, Skye grinned.

"I'm glad to hear it," Bart said.

"But I have to be honest," Leo continued. "In the end, Skye and I both know that hurt is inevitable."

"Yeah," Bart said. "The royal thing is cool, but I gotta say, I don't envy you."

"Understood. There are times I don't envy me, either."

She sighed, then headed into the living room to join them. And, hopefully, to lighten the mood. "You two talking about me?"

"No," said Bart.

"Of course," said Leo.

Bart shot him a glance. "Tattletale."

"Don't worry," Skye said, holding up her phone. "It's what all the … cool kids are doing. Here's the latest. It flashed on my notifications as I was answering Hannah's text."

She pulled it up again, then passed her phone to Bart with the headline filling the screen.

"It's L-L-Love for the P-p-pr-ince," he read. "Good grief, that's horrible. And you don't stutter."

"Right?" She held out her hands as if in exasperation. "If they're going to … make fun of me … at least get … it right."

She turned to Leo, expecting him to join in the banter. Instead, he just looked sad.

"It's … okay."

"No. It's not. I'm so sorry."

"For what? You … didn't encourage them."

"She's right," Bart said. "You're not the asshole here."

Leo's mouth twitched. "Fair enough." He reached out and ran a lock of Skye's hair through his fingers. "We should get dressed. The limo will be here within the hour."

The professor had invited them over for cocktails, and Leo had offered to rent a limo to take all three of them from the professor's home to the auditorium where he'd be receiving his award, something to which the professor had eagerly agreed.

Skye was looking forward to it, too. A limo might not be a treat for Leo, but she'd only been in one once before, after her father had rewarded her for graduating first in her law school class.

That night, she'd been crammed in with a dozen other students. Not friends so much as hangers-on. She'd kept to herself too much in law school to have made many close friends.

Tonight, she slipped into the limo with only one other person, and she felt so much more special than she had that night.

"Ever made out in a limo?" Leo asked, making her giggle.

"The driver and Jürgen can see us."

"Not anymore," he said, pushing the button to raise the privacy screen. He pulled her close and kissed her. "Thanks for coming with me."

"Are you kidding? This man is like a surrogate father to you. I'm dying to meet him."

"He's looking forward to meeting you, too. And,

unfortunately, he lives in Tarrytown," he added, his hand sliding up her thigh and under her skirt.

"That is a shame," she said, as his fingertip grazed the juncture of her thigh, tracing the elastic of her panties. "We're practically already there."

"Not quite," he said, slipping his finger under and making her gasp.

But she was right—they were almost there, and as the limo pulled in front of Professor Malkin's house, she was breathing hard. But not quite there.

"You're a tease, Your Highness."

"Just a preview of things to come. Literally," he said, his lips brushing her ear as he whispered the promise.

She giggled, then straightened her skirt just in time for Jürgen to open the door. They slipped out of the car, and she took Leo's hand as he led her up the sidewalk. The door opened as they approached, and a tall man with a graying beard stepped out to shake Leo's hand before pulling him into a fatherly hug.

"And you must be Skye," the professor said. "It's a pleasure to meet you after so long. Our Leo used to talk about you all the time."

"Did he?" She shot a mischievous glance toward Leo. "You'll have … to tell me everything he … said."

If the professor noticed her slurred speech, he

didn't show it. Instead, he simply took her arm and led her inside. "It will be my pleasure."

They only had an hour for cocktails and conversation before the limo was set to whisk them to the award venue, but within ten minutes, Skye knew it wasn't nearly long enough. She was about to say as much when Jürgen pulled Leo aside. She couldn't hear what they were saying, but she knew it was bad from the expression on Leo's face.

"What?" she asked when he returned. She put her hand on his arm and held fast, somehow certain that it would be a mistake to let him go.

"My father," he said, his voice thick with emotion. "He's had another heart attack. They don't expect him to survive. I'm so sorry, Professor. I have to go."

"Of course." Professor Malkin put his hand on Leo's shoulder. "If there's anything I can do."

"Thank you." He shook his head. "I wish there was."

"Sire," Jürgen said. "The press is already gathering."

Skye frowned, only then realizing that of course some members of the press had followed the limo to the professor's house. And if the news of the king's heart attack was public, the pack of reporters would increase exponentially by the second.

"Skye," Leo said, his hands on her shoulders. "I

have to go. I left you once without saying goodbye. This time, I'm asking you to come with me."

Her mouth went dry. Outside, she heard the clatter and shouts of the waiting press, already stifling even from behind the closed doors. She felt her chest tighten at the thought of seeing them. At having them shout out to her, even though they cared only about Leo. Of having to move through them. Speak to them.

"I … I don't think I … can. And … what would I be to you … there?" The new king's girlfriend? His mistress? She could have no role in his homeland, and they both knew it.

He touched her face. "I want to beg, my love, but I don't have time to convince you. I need to go."

She nodded, but didn't leave his side as he hurried to the door. Maybe she could do this. Maybe she could go with him, and—

Jürgen pulled the door open, and she was assaulted with the cries of reporters and the flashes of cameras. Leo turned and looked at her, and she could see from his face that he knew better than to ask again. She felt trapped. And suddenly the *deer in a headlight* expression made so much sense.

Then Leo was there, kissing her sweetly. "It's only goodbye for now," he said, though she knew that was only a platitude.

"Leo—I'm so sorry." She meant about his

father, but the words held so much more meaning than that.

He squeezed her hand. "I have to go."

She heard the pain in his voice and nodded, then bit her lip as tears started to fall. She felt the professor's hand close over her shoulder as they watched Jürgen's security team surround Leo and lead him to a waiting Town Car. Then he was gone, the limo left behind to take her and the professor on to the ceremony.

"I'm so sorry, my dear," Professor Malkin said, after he'd gently closed the door.

She managed a watery smile, then worked on her breathing until she was confident she could form words. "The multiverse," she said. "That's a … physics thing … isn't it?"

His brow furrowed, but he nodded.

"So maybe there's … another Leo and Skye … together in a universe … where I chose to go … with him."

The professor's eyes seemed as sad as her own. "Perhaps there is, my dear. But the only universe you'll know is the one you make."

Chapter Nineteen

LEO SPENT the fifteen hours on the jet from Austin to Avelle-am-see trying to sleep so that he would be awake when he saw his father. It was a fitful sleep, though, as his fear that his father would pass away before he made it home tormented Leo.

"He's not looking good," Gisele told him when they spoke on the sat phone. "I miss you, little brother."

"He can't die," Leo said. "I'm not ready to have both our parents gone."

"No one ever is," Gisele said, understanding that he meant more than just the loss of their parents. He also wasn't ready to be the king. "But we must all rise to the challenge. You, my brother, will be fine."

"Only because you'll be at my side." He closed his eyes, forcing himself not to say that it should be her who would ascend. They both knew he felt that way, just as they both knew that there was no time to push through any changes. Not unless a miracle befell their father.

"I will be wherever you need me," Gisele said. "I'll always have your back."

"I love you," he said, speaking the words in English instead of the native tongue they'd been talking in. He didn't know what possessed him, but the words made him think of Skye. Not that he'd stopped thinking of Skye. He wished she were with him, but he hadn't been surprised when she'd declined.

"I'm sorry Skye declined to come," Gisele said, making Leo smile.

"Reading my mind will be an asset since you'll be my closest advisor."

"Perhaps you are too easy to read, Your Highness."

He snorted.

"Truly," she said more gently. "I only know her through you, but I am sorry, Leo. Love isn't easy to find, and it's often harder to keep."

"Thank you," he said, wondering if his sister had ever found love. He didn't think so, and that realization made him sad. Then again, she didn't have to feel the loss he was now feeling, and he wouldn't wish that pain on anyone. "She doesn't understand the strength inside her," he said. "But I also can't blame her. She can't be my wife, and she has no desire for a public life. It's only in fairy tales that love conquers all. Usually, it's much more difficult to tame."

"You sound very wise. Just as a king should. Hurry home, brother. I'm afraid that the throne may be yours before you even arrive."

They ended the call, and he spent the remainder of the flight praying that he'd see his father one last time. His mother had died in childbirth when he'd been ten, proving to him once and for all that being a royal wasn't that special after all. How could it be when you could so easily lose the people you loved?

The airfield was twenty minutes from the palace and the royal motorcade rushed through the emptied streets, lights flashing, the nearby mountains seeming to loom in, trapping them in a nightmare. Citizens stood on sidewalks, already wearing mourning badges, and the gate around the palace was littered with flowers.

It was all too real. Too damn real.

Once they were inside the gates, he threw himself out of the car and raced up the steps and past the doormen. His footsteps echoed down the halls, then again as he pounded up the stairs. He sprinted to his father's wing, then collapsed with relief into his sister's arms.

"He's weak, but he's alive," she whispered. "Leo, I think he's waiting for you."

She pulled out of his embrace, gathering herself. Her hair was a mess, her face streaked with tears, and deep shadows accented her eyes. But she smiled at him, and he smiled back. God, he was so glad to see her.

"I need to go in."

She nodded, then hung back as he hurried to the doors as the attendants pulled them open. The doctor was at his father's bedside, and bowed when Leo came in. Leo waved off the formalities. "How is he?"

"Your father is strong," the doctor said, then lowered his voice. "You have arrived just in time, Your Highness. I am sorry."

"Leave us."

The doctor nodded, then left the room, leaving Leo alone with his father. He moved to the bed and sat on the edge.

"My son." The king's voice was barely recognizable.

"Don't try to speak, Father."

"Why not? It will do no … harm now."

Leo's heart clenched. Both at his father's words and at his cadence that reminded him of Skye. God, how he wished she were at his side.

"Don't be afraid, son," his father said. "You are

ready. And so am I. Ready to see your mother and brother again."

"I miss her," Leo said, fighting tears. "And I will miss you."

"I love you, Leopold. You and your sister. And I love this … country. Rule it well. It is hard … when the responsibility of that kind of … love rests on your shoulders. But … our small corner of … the world is at a precipice. It is … ready to move forward."

"I don't understand."

"There is … no reason … a woman cannot rule. No reason … we cannot be … a center for science … and technology."

"Father, I—" He didn't know what to say. His father had never once spoken of his children's desire that Gisele succeed their father. If he'd believed his eldest could rule, why hadn't he set those changes in motion?

"What … ever you choose, know that I … support you. You will wear the crown, my son, though I cannot say for how long. And while you … sit the throne, you will be a great leader. And one day, I hope you find a woman to sit at your side … as queen consort. For love, rather than duty." He reached out, his grip weak as he took Leo's hand. He said nothing more, his breathing turning shallow.

Leo sat with him through the long hours, and by morning, his father was dead.

Gisele had come in during the night. Now, tears streamed down her face as she rose and pulled the blanket up over their father's face.

"The King is dead," she whispered, her voice thick with tears. She met Leo's eyes. "Long live the King."

Chapter Twenty

SKYE WATCHED Leo's first press conference live on the internet. His coronation wouldn't be for another year, in a ceremony of extreme pomp and circumstance with heads of state and the country's archbishop in attendance. For now, he was "simply" ascending to the throne, having become the king from the moment of his father's death just before dawn.

In truth, though, there was nothing simple about the process, as there was plenty of to-do about the whole thing. So much, that Skye wondered if he would even have the chance to mourn.

She felt the tightness in her heart and wished that she was there with him. Not because she wanted to be in the role of girlfriend to the king—she shuddered at the thought of *that* spotlight—but because she wanted *him.* Already she missed him, wanted to comfort him. And she hated the machinations of Fate that kept them apart.

She shook it off. They were star-crossed lovers if ever there were any, but at least they'd both had their moments of bliss.

Now, Skye tapped out a quick text sending both her condolences and congratulations. She didn't even know if he would get the text. For all she knew, his phone had been only for his time in the States. Or perhaps Jürgen would screen his messages and keep this one from Leo for fear of distracting him from his duties.

Bottom line, the odds that a king would text her back were ridiculously slim, which was why her heart twisted so damn much when, five minutes after his press conference ended, she received his reply.

Thank you. I miss you. L

She released a shuddering breath and pressed the phone to her heart. Then she jumped, startled by the light tap at her bedroom door.

"It's me," Bart said. "I'm meeting Hannah and Matthew at The Fix. You should come."

"I don't know if I'm—"

"You should come," he repeated. "Come on, Skye. Sitting in here isn't going to make you feel any better. And Leo wouldn't want that for you. Neither do we."

She closed her eyes and sighed. They were right, of course. "Fine," she said, then changed out of her PJs and into real clothes before heading down to street level with Bart so they could walk the short distance to The Fix.

She'd expected looks and questions when she reached the bar. After all, the staff and many of the customers knew her—and now they knew who she'd been dating.

What she hadn't expected was the crowd gathered outside her condo.

They shouted questions as she and Bart walked, Skye keeping her head down as Bart muttered, "No comment, no comment, come on, folks, can't you give her some space?"

Finally, at the corner of Sixth and Congress, she stopped and faced them. Obviously, they weren't backing off until she said something. "I … love him. I miss … him. And I … know he'll be a … great … king."

That was all she could manage, and she was certain she sounded like an idiot, but at least she'd spoken. She owed Leo that.

"You did great," Bart assured her, hurrying her the next few blocks to the bar. Strangely enough, her comment seemed to have shut down the frenzy, and they arrived without any more demands for quotes or pictures or rudely shouted questions about how Leo was in bed. The answer was *excellent*, but that wasn't something that Skye intended to share.

"Rough walk?" Griffin asked, as he and Bev entered the bar at the same time.

"Next time, we'll take a taxi," Bart said. "Idiotic for such a short distance, but it'll at least give Skye breathing room."

"I survived," she said. "And it will … die down now that he's … King."

"Until the coronation," Bart agreed. "Then it'll start up all over again."

That was true. But that was a long way off.

Bart waved to Hannah and Matthew and started across the bar, but Skye held back, tugging Griffin to the side as Bev peeled off to sign a few autographs.

"How … do you do it?" Skye asked.

To his credit, he didn't pretend to misunderstand. He was an A-list screenwriter with a body half-covered in burns, including his face. His soon-to-be wife was an Oscar-winning actress. And he'd accepted the fact that he was going to be in the spotlight.

"I hated it for a long time," he told her. "The eyes on me. That feeling that they would think I was lesser because I didn't look the way society thought I should look, whatever that means."

"But you … own it now." She'd seen the footage from his last movie premiere. He and Bev on the red carpet, and he hadn't been wearing his signature hoodie.

He shrugged. "This is who I am. Once I accepted that it got easier."

"But how? How did you … accept it?"

He exhaled, then shrugged. "I weighed what was important over what wasn't." He ran his hand over the right side of his face. "Bev won."

"You make it sound easy."

"It wasn't," he said. "Or, it wasn't until it was."

"What changed?"

"I fell in love," he said simply. "When you let it, love makes everything easy." He smiled, only the unscarred part of his mouth curving up, then reached out to cup her shoulder. "You'll be fine, Skye."

He started to walk away, but she reached out and grabbed his sleeve. "Griff, wait."

He turned back, a question in his eyes.

"Did I make a mistake not going with him?"

He shook his head, just the tiniest of motions. "Only you know that. And if you did, well, there's this cool invention called an airplane…"

Griffin's words stayed with Skye throughout the night, so much so that she left The Fix early because she was so lost in her thoughts she got tired of asking her friends what they were talking about.

By the time she woke up, she'd made a decision, even though she hadn't actually sat down to weigh the pros and cons. It just *was*. It felt right. And once she'd decided, she knew there was no going back.

She was going to Avelle-am-see.

She wasn't going to text first. She wasn't going to ask what he wanted. That wasn't the point. This was about her—it was about owning who she was and what she wanted. About conquering her fears and taking that giant leap and every other stupid but accurate cliché she could come up with.

She was just doing it. She was just going.

And she was damn proud of herself for deciding.

Still, she couldn't take the leap without telling her father. Not only was he her boss and the only family she had, but she also loved him. He deserved to know, especially since she intended to leave the next morning, and that meant she was going to miss the symposium. A total bonus, as far as she was concerned.

There was the small problem of actually getting to Leo once she was in his country. She had a feeling that Americans weren't allowed to just enter the palace and wander freely, but she still had Jürgen's contact info. And unless Leo had told his friend and security chief that he never wanted to see Skye again, she had a feeling that Jürgen would help her. She hoped so, because without him her plan had some serious holes in it. She'd still go through with it, of course, but she'd have to come up with a Plan B.

At the moment, she was fresh out of Plan Bs.

That was something she'd worry about later, she thought as she stepped off the elevator at her father's floor. She passed reception and headed toward his office, only to see his Mary's head pop up, her eyes going wide as she saw Skye.

"Skye," she said. "What a happy coincidence. Your father just asked me to track you down. He needs to see you in his office."

"Oh." She tried to think what he could possibly need, but nothing except the symposium came to mind. She grimaced. She'd hoped to entice one of the other associates into stepping into her shoes before she officially bailed, but so far she'd found no one willing to take the bait.

"Um, right," Skye said. "So, should … I just go in?"

"Of course. He's expecting you."

She had a moment of panic—what if he freaked out when she told him her plan? But then she calmed. She was an adult. This was her life. And her dad was just going to have to support her.

She straightened her back, lifted her chin, and

pushed his office door open, determined to be cool and confident.

She froze the moment she stepped over the threshold.

He was right there.

Leo.

Just sitting in one of her dad's guest chairs in a bespoke suit, looking about as pulled together and sexy as a man could get.

She opened her mouth, shut it again, then looked at her dad. "What…?" But the word didn't come out right at all. Instead, she just whimpered some sort of question-like sound.

"Skye," Leo said, then stood. "Oh, God, Skye."

"His, ah, His Majesty has something to discuss with you," her father said, and in her crazed bewilderment, Skye almost laughed. Because when in his life had Tarlton Anderson Porter ever been befuddled?

"I'm here to hire the firm," Leo said, his eyes on Skye.

"Hire?" Her brain wasn't firing right at the moment.

"The palace would like to engage our services to consult with them on amending their constitution," her father said.

Slowly, the words gathered meaning. "I'm sorry. What?"

"His Majesty has requested that the associate

with the most expertise accompany him back to his country to work with his team in-house at the palace."

She swallowed, unable to take her eyes off of Leo. "Has he?"

"He has," Leo said. "We've been thinking many things, actually."

Her brows rose. "The royal we? Are you serious?"

"Skye!" Her father's admonition filled the room, and Skye laughed. So did Jürgen, whom she noticed by the bookcase for the first time. She glanced his way, caught his wink, and realized that the world was full of sunshine.

In front of her, Leo laughed. "Just checking. *I've* been thinking a lot of things."

"Have you?" Her voice sounded so hoarse.

He nodded toward Jürgen, who moved toward Skye's father, then whispered something. A moment later, her father caught her eye, then stepped out of the room along with the bodyguard.

She swallowed, feeling suddenly nervous. "So … um … what have you been thinking?"

"That I want you there with me, for one. That amending the constitution is a long process, and that you are uniquely qualified to help."

"I see."

"If you accept the position, you'll work with the palace legal staff—they all speak English, by the way. And when your team is ready, we'll present the amendment. If it passes, I will abdicate the throne, serving instead as both prince and science minister."

She nodded slowly, taking it all in.

Leo stood, then walked toward her. He reached out, and took her hands, and the touch of his skin against hers felt like coming home. "And, though you may not realize it," he said softly, "while the king's choices are limited, a prince can marry anyone. Even an American lawyer."

"Wow," she said. "You folks have … no standards at all."

"None," he said, and they shared a smile.

"And if the amendment doesn't pass?"

His hands tightened on hers, as if he had to hold fast against negative thinking.

"I believe it will," he said. "But if it doesn't, I won't shirk my responsibility. But as you may know, the king can marry a citizen. And it's an interesting fact that a foreigner can apply for citizenship after three years."

Her chest constricted, her skin suddenly going warm. "Is that so?"

"There's one more thing."

She swallowed. "I'm not sure I can take more." It was the truth. She was ridiculously overwhelmed.

"I'll risk it," he said, then lowered himself to

one knee as she gasped, her heart suddenly pounding in her chest.

"It turns out there is no prohibition on the king being engaged to a non-citizen. And so my darling Skye, would you do me the greatest honor and agree to marry me?"

"I—"

"It's a public life," he interrupted. "There will be speeches. State dinners. Radio addresses. But you will never be alone, and I promise the people will love you."

She didn't realize she was crying until she tasted the tears. Then all she could do was nod. "Stop trying to convince me or scare me, Leo. The answer is yes." She fell to her knees in front of him, then lost herself in his embrace.

Epilogue

Almost three years later

PRINCESS SKYE, Countess of Stahl, stood beside her husband, the former King of Avelle-am-see and its current Minister of Science. They were waiting to go inside the cathedral to take their place for Gisele's coronation.

Gisele had been ruling the small country for the last seven months since Leo had abdicated the throne the day after the constitutional amendment had been ratified. Her ascension had been a quiet affair. Today's official coronation was all about the pomp and circumstance.

"Do you regret not being Queen?" he teased.

Leo had ruled for almost two years, the time it had taken to get the amendment ratified. He and

Skye had been married seventy-two hours after he'd abdicated the throne. He'd been a popular ruler, and Skye had been shocked by her own popularity as well, both in this small country and back at home. She'd avoided public speaking as much as possible, but when she did speak, she'd had nothing but support. And when Leo had announced that he would abdicate so that his older sister could rule and so that he could marry the woman he loved, the people had cheered for him, Gisele, and Skye herself.

The foundation she'd started to help children with speech impairments was now active internationally, and Leo had made significant headway in expanding the physics department at the country's prestigious university.

Best of all, Skye was now two months pregnant, and Gisele was already planning how they would announce the impending birth of a little prince or princess to the world. A child who, if Gisele chose not to marry, might one day sit on the throne.

Now, Skye sighed happily. "What's to regret?" she asked as she leaned into Leo's embrace. "After all … I got to live the … fairy tale. And," she added, "there really is … a happily ever after."

THE END

I hope you enjoyed the story! You can read Griffin and Bev's story in Light My Fire. And don't miss Hannah and Matthew in *In Too Deep*!

Who's Your Man of the Month?

When a group of fiercely determined friends realize their beloved hang-out is in danger of closing, they take matters into their own hands to bring back customers lost to a competing bar. Fighting fire with a heat of their own, they double down with the broad shoulders, six-pack abs, and bare chests of dozens of hot, local guys who they cajole, prod, and coerce into auditioning for a Man of the Month calendar.

But it's not just the fate of the bar that's at stake. Because as things heat up, each of the men meets his match in this sexy, flirty, and compelling binge-read romance series from New York Times best-selling author J. Kenner.

"With each novel featuring a favorite romance trope—beauty and the beast, billionaire bad boys, friends to lovers, second chance romance, secret baby, and more—[the Man of the Month] series hits the heart and soul of romance." *New York Times* bestselling author Carly Phillips

Each book in the series is a STANDALONE novel with NO cliffhanger and a guaranteed HEA!

But even so, you won't want to miss any in the series. Because then you can answer the question…

Who's Your Man of the Month?

Down On Me
Hold On Tight
Need You Now
Start Me Up
Get It On
In Your Eyes
Turn Me On
Shake It Up
All Night Long
In Too Deep
Light My Fire
Walk The Line

BONUS BOOKS:
Royal Cocktail
Bar Bites: A Man of the Month Cookbook

Visit manofthemonthbooks.com to learn more!

Lovely Little Liar: Chapters 1-2

I've always loved hero-driven rom coms, especially when the guy is an alpha-hole with a bit of a marshmallow thrown in! I had such fun writing this story; I hope you enjoy the peek!

1

I don't believe in relationships, but I do believe in fucking.

Why, you ask? Hell, I could write a book. *The Guy's Guide to Financial, Emotional, and Business Success.* But honestly, why bother with a book when the thesis boils down to just four words: Don't Date. Just Fuck.

Hear me out.

Relationships take time, and when you're trying to build a business, you need to pour every spare hour into the work. Trust me on this. In the months since my buddies and I launched Blackwell-Lyon Security, we've been busting ass twenty-four/seven. Working assignments, taking meetings, building a rock solid client base.

And our commitment's paying off. I promise you our roster wouldn't be half as full as it is now if I was spending chunks of prime working time answering texts from an insecure girlfriend who was wondering why I wasn't sexting every ten minutes. So skip the dating and watch your business flourish.

Plus, hook-ups don't expect gifts or flowers. Drinks or dinner, maybe, but a guy's gotta eat anyway, right? There may be no such thing as a free lunch, but you can come close to a free fuck.

But it's the emotional upside that's the kicker for me. No walking on eggshells because she's in a bitchy mood. No feeling trapped when she demands to know why poker night was more appealing than watching the latest tearjerker starring some tanned metrosexual sporting a man bun. No wondering if she's banging another guy when she's not answering her texts.

And definitely no falling into a deep, dark pit of gloom when she breaks your engagement two weeks before the wedding because she's not sure she loves you after all.

And no, I'm not bitter. Not anymore.

But I am practical.

The truth is, I like women. The way they laugh. The way they feel. The way they smell.

I get off on making a woman feel good. On making her shatter in my arms and then beg for more.

Like them, yes. But I don't trust them. And I'm not getting fucked over again.

Not like that, anyway.

So there you go. Q.E.D.

I don't do relationships. I do hook-ups. I make it my mission to give every woman who shares my bed the ride of her life.

But it's a one-way street, and I don't go back.

That's just the way I roll. I walked away from relationships a long time ago.

So as I pull up in front of Thyme, the trendy new restaurant in Austin's upscale Tarrytown neighborhood, and hand the valet my keys, all I'm expecting is business as usual. Some causal flirting. A few appetizers. A solid buzz from a little too much liquor. And then a quick jaunt back to my downtown condo for some mid-week action.

What I get instead, is *her.*

2

"Well, then, I need you to make an announcement." The leggy brunette's voice belongs to a woman used to giving orders. "He must be here by now."

Legs is standing in front of me at the hostess stand, her back turned so that all I can see is a mass of chestnut brown waves, a waist small enough for a man to grab onto, and an ass that was made to fill out a skirt. In front of her, a petite blonde clutches a stack of menus like a lifeline as she gnaws on her lower lip.

"Well?" Legs' voice is more demand than question.

While the hostess explains to Legs that the restaurant really isn't set up for announcements, I glance at my watch impatiently. The traffic on Sixth Street had been more of a bitch than usual, and I'm running five minutes late. An irritating reality considering that I'm habitually prompt, a remnant from my military days. I'll cop to a lot of vices, but tardiness isn't among them.

Legs, however, is going to make me even later, and I frown as I glance toward the bar area to my left, looking for any unaccompanied woman who might be "J" from the 2Nite app. But there's no one sitting alone who looks like she's waiting for "PB" to join her.

It's my first time using this particular app, and its schtick—because they all have a schtick—is that all contact is anonymous until you actually meet your date. That's fine and dandy, but it makes connecting difficult. After all, would she really have left her name as J at the hostess desk? Because I'm going to feel like an idiot if I have to call myself PB.

Then again, I'll be lucky to have the chance to call myself anything at all, because Legs is spending so much time harassing the hostess that the restaurant will be closed before I can ask about J or claim a table.

"—except I already told you that I don't have his name," Legs is saying as I tune back into their conversation. The corporate warrior tone has faded, replaced by frustration and, I think, disappointment.

As for the hostess, she now looks even more frazzled.

"All I know is that he works for a security company—"

Ding, ding, ding. Folks, we have a winner.

"—and he should already be here."

"J," I say confidently, stepping up beside her. "I'm Pierce Blackwell." I pull a business card from my wallet and hand it to her when she turns to face me.

"Of Blackwell-Lyon Security. *PB*," I add, just in case that's not absolutely clear. "I'm very happy to meet you in person."

And that, frankly, is one hundred percent true. Because while the rear view might be amazing, from the front, my date for the night is even more stunning. Her dark hair frames a pale face with skin so perfect I have to force myself not to reach out and stroke her cheek. She has a wide mouth that was built for naughty things, and the kind of curvaceous body that lets a man know he has a real woman in his arms.

"Oh." Her voice is a little startled, and her amber eyes are wide with surprise. She's dropped the stern tone she'd used with the hostess, and I see relief in her eyes. I guess she thought I was going to stand her up, despite the fact that she doesn't look like the kind of woman who gets stood up often.

And her obvious relief that I've arrived suggests a vulnerability I wouldn't have guessed from listening to her interrogate the hostess.

Honestly, I like the contrast. It suggests a strong personality wrapped around a soft, feminine core. In other words, a woman who knows what she wants from a man, but isn't afraid to let him take control.

Did I mention I like taking control?

My card is still in her hand, and she glances down as she reads it, her thumb softly rubbing over the raised lettering in what I think must be an unconscious motion, but still makes me imagine the brush of that thumb over my hand, my mouth … and other much more interesting places.

She lifts her head. And in the moment she meets my eyes, I'm certain that I see a familiar spark. The kind of heat that means we skip the appetizers, slam back a quick get-to-know-you drink, then barely make it back to my condo with clothing intact.

I know women like the way I look. Dark blond hair, a body that's in prime shape at thirty-four thanks to military training and my current job's requirements, plus blue eyes that have been known to draw compliments from strangers.

So the heat I see on her face doesn't surprise me. But then I blink, and damned if that fire doesn't disappear, her eyes going completely flat. As if someone flipped a switch.

What the hell?

Was I hallucinating? Fantasizing?

Or maybe she's just doing her damnedest to fight an intense, visceral lust.

But why would she? She came here tonight wanting the same thing I did. One night. A good time. And absolutely no strings.

Honestly, it makes no sense. And right now, the only thing I'm certain of is that the desire I saw on her face is gone. *Poof.* Just like a magic trick.

No heat. No fire.

No goddamned interest at all.

"So, will that be two for dinner?" the hostess asks brightly. "The wait's about forty-five minutes in the dining room, but there are a few tables open in the bar."

"That'll be fine," I say, determined to get this evening back on track. "We'll probably stick with drinks and appetizers." I look to her for confirmation, but she's frowning at her phone and doesn't look up again until we're seated.

"The drinks here are good," I say as the hostess leaves us with the bar menus. "I live downtown, so I've been coming here a lot since it opened. How about you? Been here before?"

One perfectly groomed eyebrow arches up in a way that I find incredibly sexy, despite the fact that she's obviously annoyed. "I've only just arrived in town. When would I have had time?"

"Right. Good point." Now I'm just being conciliatory, because how am I supposed to know when she moved to Austin? I read her profile and there wasn't a single word in there about her being new to town. But my only other option is to tell her flat out that tonight is a bust, and then get the hell out of there.

Except I'm not ready to give up on her yet. Because despite our off-kilter start, there's something intriguing about J. And I know damn well that I saw a spark of interest in her eyes. And so help me, I intend to get it back. Because, hey, who doesn't love a challenge?

"Speaking of time," she says. "Under the circumstances, I feel I need to be completely honest."

"Go for it."

"It's just that I didn't appreciate being kept waiting," she says. "Punctuality is extremely important to me."

"Me too." That's true, but I'm surprised she's getting bent out of shape for a mere five minutes. Still, at least we've found one tiny patch of common ground. "I'm almost always early. I'd blame the traffic, but honestly I should have left the office earlier."

I flash my most charming smile. It hasn't failed me yet, and thankfully tonight is no exception. She relaxes a bit and leans back in her chair, her finger tracing the leather edge of the menu.

"I'm glad to hear it. You've seemed lackadaisical about the whole thing so far. It's not the attitude I'm used to."

I reach across the table and take her hand. It's soft and warm, and my cock tightens in response to a fresh wave of lust. She may be prickly and inscrutable, but she's also fiercely self-assured, and the combination is seriously hot.

"Sweetheart," I say. "I may be flippant about a lot of things, but never about this."

"Sweetheart?" She tugs her hand free of mine, and I couldn't have gone limp faster if she'd dunked me in a barrel of ice water. "And you called me *J*, too? I mean, what? Are we starting a hip hop band?"

"We could," I quip, trying to regain my balance. "PB and J. You have to admit it works."

I laugh, because it *does* work. And why the hell is she griping at me, anyway? If using initials irritates her that much, she should have picked an app other than 2Nite.

"Just call me Jez," she says. "Or Ms. Stuart if you prefer to be more formal." She's sitting up straight now, and I'm thinking that she couldn't be more formal if she tried.

"Jez," I say. "I like it."

"It's short for Jezebel, obviously. And of course our parents named my sister along the same theme." She leans back, clearly expecting a response.

"Parents will do that," I say, since I've got nothing else. Let's just say that talk of parents and siblings isn't usually par for the course on these kinds of dates.

Still, it must have been the right thing to say, because she smiles, and it's the kind of smile that lights her whole face. And even though I don't do full nights—not ever—I can't help thinking that it's the kind of smile I'd like to wake up to.

"Listen," she says, "I know I may seem formal and demanding, and that can be a little off-putting for some people. It's just that I take all of this very, very seriously."

"I get that." I mean what I say. After all, I know

that I'm a nice guy, but a woman has to be careful who she goes home with.

"I'm glad you understand," she says as the waiter comes up to take our order.

I hand the waiter my menu. "Angel's Envy. On the rocks. And the lady will have…?"

"Club soda with lime." She meets my eyes as the waiter walks away. "I like to keep a clear head."

Okay, sparks or not, this woman is exasperating. "Honestly, right now, I'm thinking I should have ordered a double."

Her mouth tightens with disapproval. "Fine. But I hope you have a clear head when it counts. I expect complete attention to detail."

I hold her gaze for ten full seconds. And then—because at this point I have nothing to lose—I slowly let my eyes roam down. Her usually full lips, now pressed together in a thin red line. The soft curve of her jaw. The tender slope of her neck.

Her top button of her silk blouse has come open, and I can see the curve of her breasts spilling out over the cups of her pale pink bra. I pause just long enough to imagine the taste of her right there. The feel of her soft skin against my lips. And the way her bossy, severe voice will soften when she writhes beneath me and begs for more.

Slowly, I raise my eyes. "Sweetheart," I say. "I'm all about the details."

I watch, satisfied, as a pink stain colors her

cheeks. She exhales, then swallows. "Right. Well, that's good."

I bite back a smile. I'm not sure what kind of game we've been playing, but there's no doubt in my mind that the score is currently in my favor.

She draws a breath, and I can tell she's trying to gather herself. "So if you're all about the details, then you already know my problem."

I lean back, grateful when the waiter returns with my drink, as that gives me time to think. *Problem?* The only problem I remember her mentioning in her profile was that she'd been working such long hours she hadn't been properly laid in months. I'd assured her I could remedy that, and she'd promptly accepted my RFD—which is 2Nite speak for "request for date."

"Well, you've been going a hundred miles an hour," I say, and she nods, looking pleased that I remember.

"And all this drama with my sister is adding a whole new layer of insanity."

"Your sister?"

She looks at me sharply, and I immediately regret my words.

"I thought you'd done your homework." There's a challenge in her voice, but I barely notice it. I'm too mesmerized by the way her lips now close over her straw.

I shift, my jeans feeling uncomfortably snug.

And honestly, what the hell? Because I can already tell this woman is bad news. Intriguing, maybe. Challenging, definitely. But way, way too much trouble.

Apparently, the parts of me below the table aren't nearly as critical, however. But I'm going to attribute that to a general desire to get laid, and not necessarily to Jez.

"Well?" she presses.

"Are you always this…" I trail off, thinking better of saying what I was thinking. *Bitchy.*

"What?"

"It's just that this smells remarkably like a job interview. Which seems a bit like overkill for just one night."

"One night? Oh, no. I'm looking for something for at least three weeks. After that, we can decide if a long term commitment would make sense."

"Wait. What?"

"I was with Larry for over five years," she says, which explains why she's been so awkward tonight. I'm guessing this is her first time to even use a dating app.

"That's quite a while," I say.

"It is. And honestly, I prefer the continuity that goes with a long-term arrangement. With someone I can trust, of course. That's what I'll be evaluating with you, of course. Assuming you check out and can prove yourself. Which, frankly, I'm starting to doubt."

I wince, suddenly picturing a panel of Olympic judges at the foot of my bed as I attempt a double rolling dismount with a flip.

I shake my head, dismissing the thought.

"Right. Okay. Let's back up." I slam back the rest of my bourbon. "Now it's my turn to call you out for being unprepared. Because my profile is crystal clear. No long term commitments." I flash that charming smile again. "Forget marriage. I'm all about the one-night stand."

"That's absurd. You're seriously considering doing this for just one night? And you think that would be okay with me? That I want to do this repeatedly?" She gestures at the table, as if having a man buy you a drink is the most hideous torture imaginable. "Are you insane?"

"My shrink doesn't think so."

She stands, then hooks her purse over her shoulder. "I wish your policy had been made clear. This has been a complete waste of time in a week when I don't have any time to waste."

"Jez—" I stand and reach for her, but she steps back. I have no idea why I want her to stay, but I do.

She, however, isn't giving me the chance to convince her.

"Thank you for the drink." She draws a breath,

and I can see her effort to settle herself. "I really am sorry for the misunderstanding. Despite everything, I think it would have been… *interesting* working with you."

And then she turns.

And then she's gone.

What the hell just happened?

"Another?" the waiter asks, as I sink back into my chair.

"Yeah. A double this time. I think I need it."

I sit there for a minute, a little shell-shocked, and I'm not sure why. I damn sure shouldn't be disappointed she walked, because that one would have been trouble for sure. The last thing I need is a woman who wants to cling.

But still, I've sat in a bar and had a drink by myself on several occasions. But never before has the empty seat across from me seemed quite so empty.

I sigh, then lift the drink the waiter slides in front of me. I savor the bite of the whiskey, wondering if it's the alcohol that's messing with my head. Making me think that maybe two dates wouldn't be the end of the world. Hell, maybe even three.

Because the truth is, even though I never quite figured her out, I haven't been that entertained by a woman in a long time.

My phone chirps, signaling an incoming message from 2Nite.

I snatch it from my jacket pocket, certain it's a message from Jez.

But it's not.

Oh, it's from J, all right. But as I read it, I get a dark, twisting feeling in my gut.

Sorry I missed our date. Work blew up and I had to fly to Dallas. Rain check?

J

I read it twice, just to make sure that the bourbon isn't making me hallucinate.

But, no. The message is clear. J—the woman I was all set to meet here tonight—isn't in Austin. She's two hundred miles away.

Which means that she didn't show.

Which means that Jez isn't J.

Which means that I have no idea who Jezebel Stuart is.

And I damn sure don't know what the hell we spent the evening talking about.

Read more in Lovely Little Liar

About the Author

J. Kenner (aka Julie Kenner) is the *New York Times*, *USA Today*, *Publishers Weekly*, *Wall Street Journal* and #1 International bestselling author of over one hundred novels, novellas and short stories in a variety of genres.

Visit www.jkenner.com to subscribe to JK's newsletter and visit her social media!

Stay in touch with JK and be the first to know about new releases: **Just text: JKenner to 21000 to subscribe to JK's text alerts.**

Made in the USA
Monee, IL
26 July 2021

74285914R00118